PRAISE FC

Mimi Matthews

The Lost Letter

"The perfect quick read for fans of Regency romances as well as Victorian happily-ever-afters, with shades of Austen and the Brontës that create an entertaining blend of drama and romance."

-*RT Book Reviews*

"A fast and emotionally satisfying read, with two characters finding the happily-ever-after they had understandably given up on. A promising debut."

-*Library Journal*

A Holiday By Gaslight

"Matthews (*The Matrimonial Advertisement*) pays homage to Elizabeth Gaskell's *North and South* with her admirable portrayal of the Victorian era's historic advancements … Readers will easily fall for Sophie and Ned in their gaslit surroundings."

-Library Journal, starred review

"Matthews' novella is full of comfort and joy—a sweet treat for romance readers that's just in time for Christmas."

-Kirkus Reviews

"A graceful love story...and an authentic presentation of the 1860s that reads with the simplicity and visual gusto of a period movie."

-Readers' Favorite

The Matrimonial Advertisement

"For this impressive Victorian romance, Matthews (*The Viscount and the Vicar's Daughter*) crafts a tale that sparkles with chemistry and impresses with strong character development...an excellent series launch … "

-Publishers Weekly

"Matthews (*The Viscount and the Vicar's Daughter*) has a knack for creating slow-building chemistry and an intriguing plot with a social history twist."

-Library Journal

"Matthews' (*The Pug Who Bit Napoleon*, 2018, etc.) series opener is a guilty pleasure, brimming with beautiful people, damsels in distress, and an abundance of testosterone ... A well-written and engaging story that's more than just a romance."

-Kirkus Reviews

The Viscount and the Vicar's Daughter

"Matthews' tale hits all the high notes of a great romance novel ... Cue the satisfied sighs of romance readers everywhere."

-Kirkus Reviews

"Matthews pens a heartfelt romance that culminates into a sweet ending that will leave readers happy. A wonderfully romantic read."

-RT Book Reviews

The LOST LETTER

A Victorian Romance

MIMI MATTHEWS

THE LOST LETTER
A Victorian Romance

Cover Design by James T. Egan of Bookfly Design
Interior Book Design & Typesetting by Ampersand Book Interiors

E-Book: 978-0-9990364-0-2
Paperback: 978-0-9990364-1-9

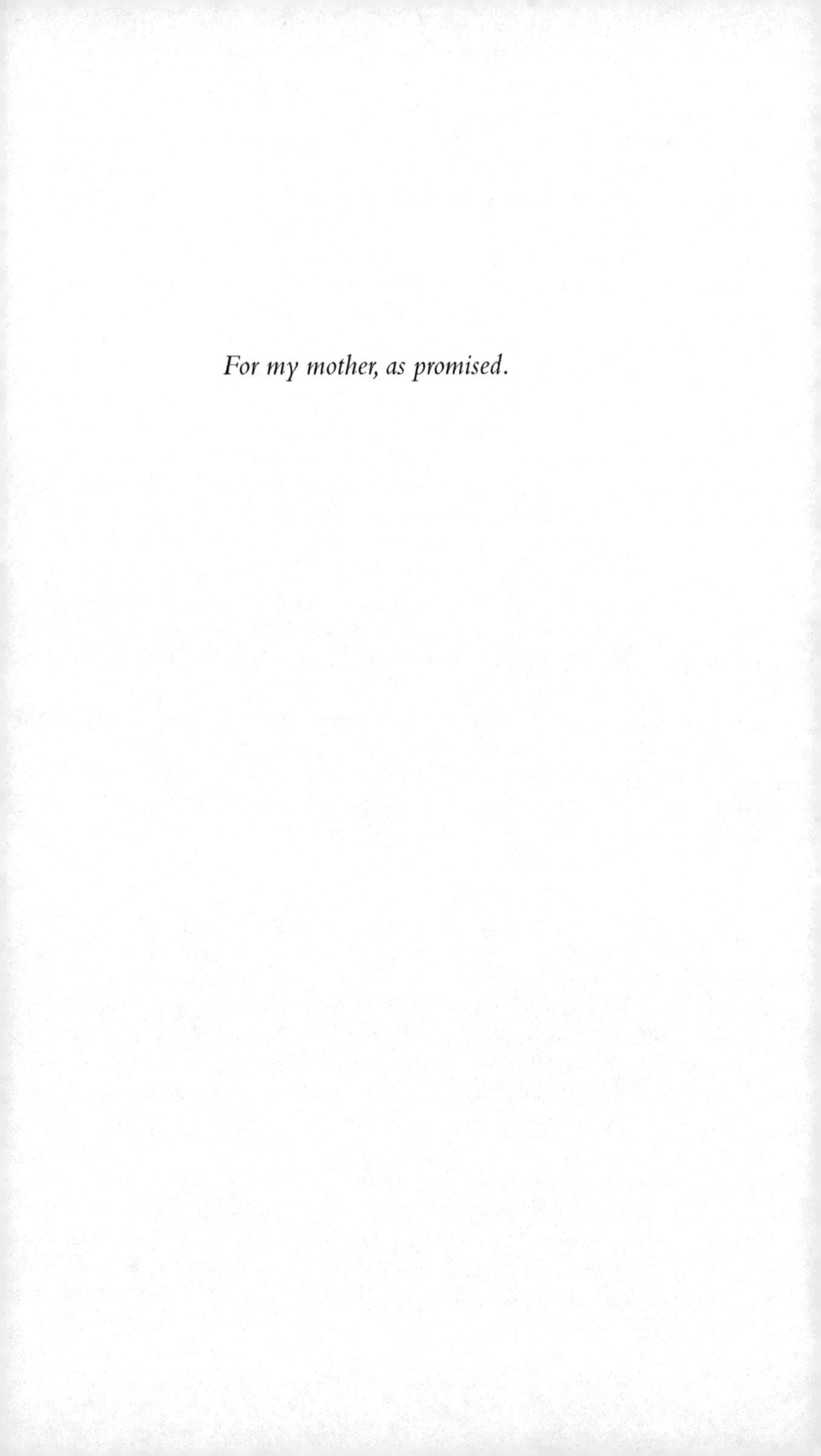

For my mother, as promised.

Chapter One

London, England
Spring, 1860

Sylvia Stafford smoothed out the skirts of her plain, dark gray gown as she followed her employer, Mrs. Dinwiddy, down the stairs. She was not strictly forbidden to receive callers; however, in her entire two years as governess to the Dinwiddy children, no friends or family had ever attempted to call upon her. Not that there were a great deal of either in her life at the moment. After her father's suicide, the only family remaining had been a parcel of disapproving aunts and uncles. And any society friends she might have had in her role as Miss Stafford of Newell Park in Kent had all since long disappeared.

"I do not know a Lady Harker," she said. "At least, I do not *think* I do. It is very possible we may have met once, long ago."

"She was very insistent," Mrs. Dinwiddy replied.

"You spoke with her, ma'am?"

"Oh yes. We had a nice little chat." Mrs. Dinwiddy gave a chortle of laughter. "Imagine me! Chatting with a viscountess of all things! But she's only a young lady and pleasant enough for all her finery. She put me quite at my ease."

The Dinwiddy's modest parlor, like the rest of their house in Cheapside, was both tasteful and comfortable. Sylvia entered it to find a smallish woman perched on the edge of an armless, button-back chair, her fashionably flounced skirts draped over a wire crinoline of truly magnificent proportions. She *was* young. Younger at least than Sylvia's own five and twenty years. And she had a vaguely harried expression, complimented rather comically by a frothy lace and ribbon cap, pinned slightly askew, atop a profusion of blond curls.

She sprang from her seat, her large brown eyes immediately fixing on Sylvia. And then she smiled. "You are Miss Stafford?" She strode forward. "I recognized your hair! How lovely it is. And how lovely *you* are, too! I do thank you for bringing her so quickly, Mrs. Dinwiddy. Is it possible I might speak with her alone?"

Mrs. Dinwiddy was a kind employer and readily acceded to Lady Harker's request, even volunteering to have tea sent in.

"I feel I should remember you, Lady Harker," Sylvia said after her employer had withdrawn from the room, "but I fear I do not."

Lady Harker's smile faded. "No, indeed. We have never met, Miss Stafford. Oh, but I am so happy to have found you. You cannot know..."

Sylvia was alarmed to see tears starting in Lady Harker's eyes. "My dear ma'am," she said gently, "please have a seat. And pray take my handkerchief. Here. Do you see the little knots of blue and brown thread? It is one of the first efforts of Miss Dinwiddy at embroidery. They are meant to be flowers. She gave this handkerchief to me last Christmas. It was wrapped around a cake of my favorite violet scented soap."

Once upon a time, Sylvia had been admired for her velvety voice. It was low and soft. Seductive, one ardent suitor had said. Indeed, there was seldom a London party during which, at some point, she had not been begged to sing. Now, however, her voice was an exceedingly practical attribute, used daily to soothe her young charges and nightly to read or sing them to sleep. It was also invaluable for calming the perpetually flustered cook, the worried housemaid, and anyone else whose nerves were out of balance.

It worked just as well on highly-strung aristocrats.

Distracted, Lady Harker sank into a chair, her attention focused on the collection of misshapen knots of thread that bordered the handkerchief. "Miss Dinwiddy is the child you teach here?"

Sylvia seated herself in the chair across from Lady Harker, her own full skirts settling about her in a moderate spill of serviceable gray wool. "Yes, ma'am. Miss Clara Dinwiddy is the eldest daughter of the house. She is eight now. I also teach her younger sister, Cora. Cora is six."

"I had not thought to find you a governess," Lady Harker said as she blotted her eyes.

Sylvia was not offended. If truth be told, she had not thought to find herself a governess either. She had expected to marry. There had even been a special gentleman once. A gentleman who had come far closer to winning her hand than any other suitor. But Papa's suicide had changed everything. The family she had been staying with for the London season could not bustle her back to the country soon enough. And after that, she had never heard from any of her suitors again.

Not that any of that mattered now. Her tears had long since dried up and the part of her which had once dreamed impossible romantic dreams had withered and died. She was not unhappy now. Far from it. She laughed easily and often. She never thought of her old life anymore. Well, almost never.

"The Dinwiddys have been very good to me," she said truthfully. "I count myself lucky to have found a position with them."

Lady Harker flushed. "Oh, I did not mean to insult you! It is only that I expected you would be married with children of your own. Lady Medcalf told me that you had so many admirers before…" Her flush deepened. "But I must say, I am glad to find you unattached. More glad than I can say."

Sylvia smiled. "Perhaps you had better tell me why you have come."

"Yes. Yes, of course." Lady Harker grew instantly solemn. "Well…you see, Miss Stafford…my elder brother is a very difficult man."

Sylvia nodded with understanding, unperturbed by this non sequitur.

"He has always been difficult. So stern and grave. We were never very close. He is so much older than I am. But while he was away in India, my father and eldest brother died of fever. And now he is the only family I have left. Indeed, he is the head of the family, for he has the title now. Not that I must put up with his moods. My husband will not permit me to stay with my brother above a fortnight. He fears he may be violent. But he has never been violent with me, Miss Stafford. Well…" She twisted the handkerchief in her hands. "Perhaps he has thrown a book and once he did throw a porcelain figure, but he was not trying to hit me with them. He was only trying to scare me."

Sylvia listened with calm attention. She had become used to hearing long nonsensical tales from her charges. She prided herself on her patience.

"He would not hurt a woman," Lady Harker continued. "It is just these moods of his. He becomes so overwrought, you see. One night, last month, I thought I heard him calling out. I went to his room. Just to peep in at him. And he was sitting in his chair with his head in his hands and he was *crying*. I did not know what to do! I tried to comfort him, but he said I must get out or he would wring my neck." She reddened. "That is when I first saw it. He had it clasped in one of his hands. He was holding it whilst he was weeping."

Lady Harker took a breath. "Well, I thought I must have imagined it. The next day, I checked all round his room, but I could not find it. I was near giving up when it occurred to me that I should question his valet." She beamed with obvious pride at this decision. "His valet, Milsom, was his batman during the uprising. He is ridiculously loyal to my brother. Naturally he refused to tell me anything. But I scolded him like a very fury. At last, he said that it was indeed a lock of hair. That my brother had carried it with him to India. As a talisman."

The demeanor of gentle encouragement with which Sylvia had listened to Lady Harker's story thus far noticeably slipped. "I am sorry, ma'am. Did you say a *lock of hair*?"

"Yes. A thick lock of dark brown hair. Milsom confessed that it belonged to a lady named Miss Sylvia Stafford and that—"

Sylvia felt all the color drain out of her face. A long suppressed memory threatened to overwhelm her. "You don't mean that your brother…That your brother is…"

"The Earl of Radcliffe. Though you would have known him as Colonel Sebastian Conrad—Oh dear! Miss Stafford!" Lady Harker leapt up and rushed to Sylvia's side. "Have you swooned? Shall I fetch my *sal volatile*? Do say something Miss Stafford!"

Sylvia stared up at the chattering figure of Lady Harker. "I have not swooned," she said. "I am perfectly well. Only a little surprised."

Lady Harker clasped Sylvia's hand. "My dear Sylvia…May I call you Sylvia? And you must call me Julia, for I feel as if you are a sister to me already. And I mean to make you my sister. It is why I have come. To force you back to Hertfordshire with me so that you may marry my brother and make him well again. But I mustn't get ahead of myself. We must first get to know each other and then—Ah! Here is our tea."

She released Sylvia's hand to usher in the maid with the tea service. Having done so, she sent her back out again, sat down, and proceeded to pour. "Sugar? Lots of it?" She dropped several lumps into Sylvia's teacup and stirred briskly. "Here you are, Miss Stafford. A few sips of this and you shall feel better directly."

Sylvia took the teacup with visibly trembling hands. She forced herself to take a swallow. The hot, sweet liquid calmed her quivering insides, but she did not think there was a beverage on earth that could calm her quaking heart. "Your brother…" she began, amazed that her voice was as steady as it sounded. "You say that he was injured in India?"

Lady Harker heaved a sigh. "Horribly injured, I'm afraid." She helped herself to a chocolate biscuit. "A saber cut cleaved the side of his face and he is now terribly scarred and blind in one eye. He did not lose the eye, thank goodness. It is only cloudy. I say this to prepare you, Miss Stafford. For when I first beheld him, I am afraid I acquitted myself rather badly. It is a bit frightening, you see."

Sylvia slowly lowered her teacup back to its saucer and returned them both to the tea tray. She was trembling all over now and hard pressed to conceal it. "Is your brother in very much pain?" she asked faintly.

"I fear so. Though, I do think he could bear it all better if he would only allow people to come and see him." She heaved another sigh. "But he does not want anyone to see him. I think he is ashamed to have lost his looks. Not that he was ever very handsome to begin with. But I daresay you thought he was, else why would you have given him such a large lock of your hair?"

Sylvia thought of that night in Lord and Lady Mainwaring's garden so long ago. The air had been redolent with the perfume of roses. The stars shining like diamonds. She had let him kiss her there. And she had kissed him in return, cradling his stern jaw in her hands. "*How many young ladies have you kissed in moonlit gardens, I wonder,*" she had murmured to him.

"*None but you, Miss Stafford,*" he had replied huskily. "*None but you.*"

Sylvia looked across at Lady Harker. She could see no resemblance between her and Colonel Conrad. Sebastian had been tall, dark, and broad-shouldered, his features harsh, as if carved from granite. He had been intimidating to most. Especially to young, silly women. Sylvia's friends had gasped behind their fans when first he approached her and asked her to dance.

"*You've frightened them,*" she had told him. Indeed, except for a brief introduction at a party the previous evening, those may have been the very first words she had ever spoken to Sebastian Conrad.

"*Have I?*"

"*They are all about to swoon.*"

He had stared down at her, an expression in his eyes hard to read. "*But not you, I take it.*"

"*Oh, I never swoon. And it takes a great deal to frighten me. Far more than a scowl.*" She had smiled up at him then, adding, "*You shall have to try harder, sir.*"

Sylvia hated to think of it now. "Yes, I did give him a lock of my hair," she said. "It was very wrong of me to do so. We were not engaged. And we had no understanding between us. But I was young then, poorly chaperoned, and I confess, far too romantic minded for my own good."

"Never say so, Miss Stafford! Your lock of hair has given him ever so much comfort. And I am sure he meant to propose. You must know that words have never come easily to my brother. And I have never known him to even speak with a young woman—unless you count that gruff sort of grumbling he was always used to do. Why, you could have knocked me over with a feather when I discovered that he had a lock of hair from his sweetheart. If I had only known—"

"Lady Harker—" Sylvia objected.

"Naturally, I wrote to all my friends to find out who you were and where you were. I told my husband that if I had not found you by Christmas, I would hire a private enquiry agent to do so. But as luck would have it, my dear friend Lucinda Cavendish was staying with Lord and Lady Ponsonby in London and was able to discover from Lady Ponsonby's maid, Miss Button, that you—"

"*Button*? My former lady's maid?" Sylvia was stunned. She had not thought of Button in ages, but the mere mention of her name was enough to bring it all back.

Papa had hired Miss Button to be her lady's maid just after her fifteenth birthday. She had been one of the only constants in Sylvia's young life. How well she could remember Button arranging her hair as she sat in front of her ornately gilded dressing table. Or Button waiting up until all hours to help her undress and to listen, avidly, as she related everything that had happened at whichever ball or concert she had been attending that evening. Button had even been the one to comfort her on those rare occasions when something—or someone—had driven her to tears.

And yet, for all that, she and Button had never been more than mistress and servant. It was a fact which had been painfully driven home to her in the days following Papa's suicide.

"*What shall we do, Button?*" she had wept during the initial, overwhelming wave of grief. "*What is to become of us?*"

But there was no *us*. The ink had hardly been dry on Sir Roderick's death certificate before Button was informing her that she had secured a new place and would be taking her leave.

Sylvia had known herself then to be truly alone.

"That's right." Lady Harker nodded. "Miss Button said that you had gone into service with a family named Dinwiddy as governess to their children. It was not long after that I found you here in Cheapside."

"I see." Sylvia looked down at her hands as they lay folded in her lap. They were chalk white. Rigid. "Does your brother know that you have come here?" she asked, raising her gaze back to Lady Harker's face.

"Lord no! I mean to surprise him. And once we have you settled in the house, he cannot very well turn you away—"

"*I beg your pardon?*"

"That is, if you will be so good as to come with me to Hertfordshire for two weeks. I am to stay at Pershing Hall. My brother is there all alone now, but I do try to visit as frequently as I can and it is quite unexceptionable for me to bring a guest."

Sylvia's heart was thundering madly. It was a physical pain in her chest, the likes of which she had not felt in years. "Lady Harker—"

"Oh please, call me Julia!"

"Julia. You must see that I cannot accept your invitation."

"Why ever not? Your employer tells me that you have never taken a holiday and she has already agreed I might take you away with me for as long as a month. And it is not as if you will be alone with my brother. I will be present in the house and, in a fortnight, my husband will join me there. It will be quite respectable, I assure you."

Sylvia could only imagine the reception she would receive from Sebastian after all of these years. To arrive uninvited at his home, poor as a church mouse and tainted by the scandal of her father's suicide? As if she were a beggar seeking favor from him? "I cannot," she said again. "I simply cannot. It would be too painful for me. Pray do not ask me again, ma'am."

Lady Harker's face crumpled. "But you cannot refuse me, Miss Stafford! You are the only hope for my brother to get well!"

"No, ma'am." Sylvia rose from her chair on unsteady legs. "You are mistaken. Your brother does not care for me."

Lady Harker leapt up. "But the lock of hair—"

"A token, nothing more. Many soldiers keep such, I understand."

"No. No. I will not believe it. I have come all this way. I beg you, Miss Stafford. If the lock of hair brings him comfort, only think what you might do if you were to come in person." She clasped Sylvia's hand. "You do not have to marry him. I should never have said that. It is only my foolish fancy. But do come. Please. Just to see him. If he shouts at you or threatens you, I shall have my coach convey you straight back to London." Tears were rising in her eyes. "Do come," she begged. "If things do not change for my brother soon, I fear he will do something stupid."

The words went through Sylvia like an electric current. "Something stupid? What do you mean?"

"Oh, but you must know what I mean, Miss Stafford. You *must* know."

Sylvia shook her head in disbelief. Her own father's suicide was a wound that would never fully heal. The very idea that Sebastian would be considering a similar course was too horrible to contemplate. She had cared for him so deeply once. Only the passage of time had numbed the pain and hurt left after he had gone away and forgotten her. "Has he threatened to do himself harm?" she asked.

"No," Lady Harker admitted slowly. "Though he does keep his pistol out in his room. I have seen it near his bedside. He has kept it there this whole year. It is awfully upsetting. And my husband says I should not be upset at the moment. I am in an interesting condition, you see, and if something were to happen to my brother..."

The last of Sylvia's defenses crumbled. No matter how cruelly Sebastian had treated her in the past, he did not deserve to be suffering in such a dreadful manner. No one did. If her presence could alleviate even a fraction of his pain, she must go to him. It would be hardhearted to continue refusing. Far worse, it would be cowardly. "Very well," she said.

Lady Harker's mouth curved into a wobbly smile. "Do you mean you will come?"

"Yes. I will come away with you. If...If you truly believe it will help him."

Lady Harker flung her arms around Sylvia in an impulsive embrace. "Oh, thank you. Thank you. You will not be sorry. I promise you."

Sylvia heard Lady Harker's tearful exclamations as if she were standing somewhere far outside of her body. She heard herself agreeing to go with Lady Harker that very day. Agreeing to pack her things so they might leave immediately. Lady Harker summoned Mrs. Dinwiddy and the two of them briefly conversed as well.

"A little holiday with some of your old friends," Mrs. Dinwiddy said to Sylvia, smiling. "You must take the month, Miss Stafford. I insist upon it."

Before she knew it, Sylvia was in her small upstairs bedroom, carefully packing her things into a well-worn carpetbag.

Only then did she come to her senses, a swell of panic building in her chest, threatening to suffocate her.

She was not a coward. She had handled everything these last two years with grace and dignity. All the slights, the cruel remarks, and even the cut direct from Penelope Mainwaring, a girl whom she had once considered to be her best friend in the whole world. But now, the very idea of seeing Sebastian Conrad again frightened her to the marrow of her bones.

She had loved him. She could admit that to herself without rancor. She had loved him and she had thought, for a very little while, that he had loved her. He had never said so, of course. Neither had he made her any promises. But he had sought her out at every ball, managed to cross her path whenever she was out walking or riding, and even, on two occasions, miraculously appeared at Hatchard's book shop when she needed to reach a book from a shelf that was too high.

Then, after that last night in the garden, he had gone. Suddenly. Ordered back to India to assist in suppressing the rebellion of 1857. He had never responded to her letters. And he had never written to her in return. Not even a brief note of condolence a year later when her father died. She had simply never heard from him again. For a time, she had even feared that he was dead, but his name was not listed in any of the newspaper reports that she read so obsessively.

Eventually, she had come to grips with the fact that he had forgotten her. It had taken a long while, but she was content again. Happy in her position. Happy in her life. She had remade herself into someone stronger. Someone who could not be hurt again. Or so she hoped. She had never had to put it to the test—until now.

Was he truly so badly scarred? And in so much pain? She hated to imagine it. And she hated herself for wanting so badly to go to him, to comfort him and lend him aid.

So he had kept that ridiculous lock of her hair. What did that signify? It did not mean that he wanted her. That he missed her. They had hardly known each other, after all. It had been a few months during the season. A few whispered conversations. A few lingering looks. A few kisses.

She changed into a modest travelling costume, assessing herself in the small mirror above her washstand as she buttoned her mantle at her neck. Did she look the same as she had then? It was little more than three years. Not much about her could have changed, surely. She still had the same thick, glossy chestnut hair. The same wide blue eyes and dimpled cheeks. And her figure was much the same, too. Still shapely in a subdued sort of way, with long legs and a slender waist.

Yet somehow she did not look the same at all. Had being a governess turned her into a drab? She would not go that far. But there was definitely a somberness to her now. A lack of that subtle sparkle which had once made her stand out from the other young ladies.

Well, she may have lost her sparkle, but it sounded as if Sebastian Conrad had very nearly lost his mind. He would be in no position to judge her for her looks. And if he said a single word in criticism of her for being a governess or made a single unkind remark about her father, she would tell him exactly what she thought of faithless gentlemen who compromised young ladies in gardens and then abandoned them.

Chapter Two

Hertfordshire, England
Spring, 1860

Sebastian Conrad, Earl of Radcliffe, raised his head from his book at the unmistakable sound of a carriage arriving. Despite his injuries, his hearing was as acute as it had ever been. He could easily make out the crunch of wheels on gravel, the sound of doors opening and closing, and following it all, the high-pitched laughter of his younger sister, Julia.

He scowled deeply.

Pershing Hall was a huge, architectural nightmare of a house, filled with meandering corridors, rooms of varying sizes, and passageways that led to nowhere. But when his sister, Julia, Viscountess Harker, was present, the house seemed to shrink to a fraction of its size.

There was no peace and quiet. No privacy. Sebastian already lived in almost complete seclusion in the earl's apartments. When Julia was in residence, however, he felt as if he were a prisoner there.

She had last visited only a month ago. Why was she back so soon? To devil and torment him, no doubt.

"Milsom!" he shouted.

His throat had been partially damaged by a saber cut, rendering his voice a particularly harsh, rasping growl. At the sound of it, his former batman materialized at the door of the dressing room. A rangy fellow with a sharp, foxlike face, he was two and thirty, the same age as Sebastian, but somehow managed to look as if he were decades older.

"My lord?" he queried.

"Lady Harker is here. Again."

Milsom knew better than to question his master's superior hearing. "Shall I lay out a fresh suit of clothes, my lord?"

Sebastian's shoulder and arm ached. The last thing he wanted to do was truss them up in a blasted coat. Nor why should he have to? He was under no obligation to play lord of the manor. He had not invited his sister here. If she insisted upon forcing her presence upon him, she could bloody well bear to look at him in his shirtsleeves. "Unnecessary," he said.

Milsom surveyed him with a critical eye. "Shall I shave you, my lord?"

Sebastian's beard grew erratically on the side of his face that was scarred, but on the left side he had a good two-day growth of black stubble. He looked monstrous enough when clean-shaven, he knew. With facial hair, he looked a veritable beast. "No," he said coldly.

There was no need. He likely would not even see his sister.

He returned his attention to his book, but could not settle back into reading. The presence of other people in the house always made him uneasy. And, much as he loved her, he could scarcely tolerate the visits of his younger sister. She was too loud. Too emotional. Too cursed intent on interfering in his life.

She meant well, but she had no real notion of what he had been through in India. Nor could he ever confide in her. Like so many young ladies of her class, she was a coddled innocent who swanned through life clutching a vinaigrette lest she swoon away at the first sign of something unpleasant.

She had swooned when she had first beheld him, hadn't she? Screamed, swooned, and then burst into tears—in that order. As if he had not felt hideous enough.

He tightened his fingers around the lock of hair in his hand. Even after all of these years it was still as soft as silk. He caressed it absently with his thumb, the familiar action calming him enough that he was able to resume reading. He heard Milsom milling about behind him, tidying up the sitting room.

"You'll give yourself a headache, my lord," he remarked.

Sebastian made no reply. Reading was one of his only pleasures now and even that was marred by frequent headaches. The strain of reading with one eye, the doctor had said. Confound him.

Before being injured, Sebastian's leisure hours had been taken up with riding and sport and scholarship. He had even penned several articles for *The Aristotelian Review*—a somewhat obscure scholarly journal focused on classicalism and antiquity. His primary occupation, however, had been as a soldier. It was the career path chosen for all the second sons of the Earls of Radcliffe, and it was a life that suited Sebastian particularly well. He had always been an ordered and disciplined individual with a serious turn of mind. Rather too serious, he had been told on occasion.

But he had not lacked for courage. And though he did not relish fighting and bloodshed, he had found himself to be extraordinarily adept at it.

He had expected to eventually come home from India to the modest property that his father had given him for his twenty-first birthday. Instead he had had his face nearly cleaved in two and returned to England to find his father and his elder brother dead. In place of a modest property, he now had a substantial estate. And instead of a second son, he was now the Earl of Radcliffe.

Fortunately, his younger sister had been married off to the Viscount Harker two years prior and was no longer Sebastian's concern. And Pershing Hall itself was in the very capable hands of his father's steward, a man who had managed the estate for over thirty years.

Sebastian was content to leave it to him.

He could muster no interest in poring over ledgers and even less in riding out to meet with any of the tenants. It was too easy to imagine their horrified reaction to the sight of his scarred face. Granted, he had known most of his father's tenants since his youth, but mere familiarity was no guarantee that they would not respond to him with pity and disgust. He need only look to his sister's reaction for proof of that.

"That'll be Lady Harker now," Milsom said.

Sebastian stiffened at the sound of muffled footsteps coming up the stairs and down the hall. The housekeeper, Julia, and one other. Lord Harker, perhaps? Good God, he hoped not. The last time that pompous ass had come to visit him in his rooms it was to read him an officious lecture on why a gentleman must never threaten to throttle his sister. But no, it was clearly the housekeeper and two women. Julia and her maid. Or Julia and a friend. Heaven help him. How long did his sister plan to stay?

"I am not receiving, Milsom," he informed his hovering valet.

"Naturally, my lord," Milsom replied. And when a gentle tap—the sort of anemic knock one might give at an invalid's door—announced the presence of his irritating younger sibling, Sebastian heard Milsom open the door a crack and say, quite firmly, "His lordship's not receiving today, my lady."

"Not receiving! Look here Milsom..." Julia's voice sunk to a poor apology of a whisper. "We discussed this and you promised that you would be of some assistance! If you care at all for my brother you will let me pass!"

Sebastian heard a rustle of expensive fabric as Julia shouldered past his valet and stormed into the room. With a sigh of resignation, he rose from his chair and turned to face her.

And then he froze.

The door to his room stood open. Julia was striding toward him, Milsom standing by the door with a helpless look on his face. And in the hall, her wide, blue eyes meeting his from across the distance, was Sylvia Stafford.

Sebastian felt, all at once, as if all the breath had been knocked out of his body.

He would know her face anywhere. It had been emblazoned on his brain through every icy cold night, every sweltering march, and every bloody skirmish. It was the last thing he had seen before he lost consciousness in the dirt outside the gates of Jhansi. The one image he had clung to when he was certain that he was about to die.

And now here it was before him. That lovely, long treasured face. A perfect oval, sculpted by fine cheekbones, a straight, elegant nose, and a soft, voluptuous mouth. He had kissed that mouth once. A lifetime ago. And those slender hands that were now clutching white-knuckled to her bonnet had once caressed his face.

"*May I have a lock of your hair, Miss Stafford*?" he had asked her the last night they were together. He remembered it as clearly as if it had happened yesterday. It had been at a ball given by Lord and Lady Mainwaring. He had taken her out for a walk in the garden. There had been a full moon.

"*You may,*" she had said, blushing. "*But I'm afraid you must cut it yourself.*"

Her thick, chestnut hair had been swept up in a spray of sapphires. He had touched it for the first time with an unsteady hand, working loose a single glossy curl with his finger. "*Is this all right?*"

"*It feels like rather a lot. Perhaps you might take a bit less?*"

"*I shall take so much,*" he had said, neatly severing the lock with a small pocketknife, "*that there will be nothing left for you to give to your other admirers.*"

She had looked up at him with a quizzical smile. "*Do you imagine I oblige every gentleman who requests a lock of my hair?*"

"*Have other gentlemen made such a request?*"

"*Yes.*"

"*And have you…?*"

"*No,*" she had said. "*You are the first.*" And then she had carefully removed one of the pale blue silk ribbons from her gown and given it to him to bind up the freshly cut tresses. "*What will you do with it?*" she had asked him afterward.

"*Keep it close to my heart,*" he had replied gravely. "*And whenever I despair of coming home again, I shall take it out and look at it. And I shall think of you.*"

Sebastian felt a tremor go through him. But it was not merely an effect of the deeply unhappy memory. It was part rage. Part horror. He had been standing, staring at her, showing her his full face. For how long? One second? Two seconds? Enough time for her to have a clear view of his sightless eye and of every wretched scar. He turned away, his hand raising instinctively to cover the right side of his face.

And then Milsom shut the door.

"You mustn't be angry, Sebastian!" Julia approached with hands clasped beseechingly to her bosom. "If you will let me explain—"

"By God, I should wring your neck," he rasped. "And you." He turned on his traitorous valet. "Curse and confound you—"

"Pray don't blame Milsom! I forced him to tell me about her. He had no choice."

Sebastian could hear the housekeeper in the hall offering to show the young lady to her room. Footsteps sounded as the two walked away. He listened intently for Miss Stafford's distinctive voice, deeply ashamed of himself for needing so desperately to hear it, but there was only silence.

"And you cannot blame me," Julia continued. "For once I learned about the lock of hair that you keep I could not rest until I knew the entire story."

Sebastian's scarred face went white with fury. He looked from Milsom to Julia and back again. What the devil had his valet told his meddling sister? More importantly, what in hell had his sister told to Miss Stafford? "Get out," he snarled, advancing on her.

Julia retreated behind a chair. "I've persuaded her to stay the month," she said. "It was the best I could manage. She cannot stay any longer than that because of the children, you see, and—"

"*What*?"

Julia offered him a tentative smile. "Two little girls."

Sebastian went still. Once again he had the sense of all the breath leaving his body. "Their father?" he managed to ask.

"Mr. Claude Dinwiddy. A merchant. Can you imagine?"

He sank blindly back into his chair, managing to find it beneath him by only the purest chance. He leaned his head back against the leather upholstery, breathing raggedly as his fingers closed tightly around the lock of hair hidden in his hand.

Why had he never thought…? Never considered…? Of course she was married! Of course she had children! And why in God's name should it matter anymore? It had been three years since he had known her. If he had ever known her.

She was nothing to him now.

"My lady, if you'll give us a moment," Milsom murmured to Julia.

Ignoring the valet, Julia came to perch on the chair opposite from her brother. "Is it the pain, Sebastian? Does it hurt very terribly? Oh, do something Milsom!"

Milsom already had the matter well in hand. "Here you are, sir," he said. "Just as you like it."

Sebastian opened his eyes, to find the familiar face of his batman looming over him. He was holding out a glass of brandy and a folded handkerchief. Sebastian took both, using the handkerchief to press against the injured side of his mouth as he drank. The nerves had deadened there and he had learned early on that, unless he made some effort to prevent it, liquid would leak out of his mouth and run straight down his chin.

Julia began to weep. "I am sorry. I did not mean to make things worse. Shall I send her back, Sebastian? Please do not make me. It was ever so difficult to convince her to come. And she has been given the whole month to stay here. Pray let her, Sebastian. It is the only holiday poor Miss Stafford has had in two years!"

For once, Sebastian did not trust his hearing. "*Miss* Stafford?"

"Certainly Miss Stafford! Whom did you think I meant? Oh, dear! You have not become confused, have you? Is it from the pain? Or is it—"

Milsom cleared his throat. "If I may interject, my lady. You've given the impression that Miss Stafford is married to a Mr. Dinwiddy—"

"I never did! I said she was a governess to the Dinwiddy family." Julia paused, her brow creasing. "Didn't I?"

"A governess," Sebastian repeated. "I don't believe it."

"Oh, but it is true! That is where I found her. At a quaint little house in Cheapside. She had no idea who I was at first, but after I explained...Well...She did not want to come—"

"No doubt," he said acidly, taking another swallow of his brandy.

"Not because of your injury. I think...That is... She said that I was mistaken. That you did not care for her. Though I do not know how that can be since you have kept her lock of hair with you all this time. And so I told her!"

"You *what*?"

Julia drew back. "I know I should not have said so, but she would not have believed you wanted to see her otherwise, would she? I daresay she is disappointed you did not come to her aid after her father died."

Anger, mortification, and deep, overwhelming misery warred within his breast. He scarcely knew what his sister said anymore. Miss Stafford was not married? Miss Stafford was a governess? Her father was dead?

He had been home nearly a year, secluded in the country and, most of the time, very nearly off his head with pain and anguish. He had not been able to bear the daily papers. Indeed, the British Army, the sepoy rebellion, and the entire continent of India had been topics on which no one at Pershing Hall dared utter a word. As a result, he had missed the news of marriages, births, and deaths. He had grown entirely disconnected from the world he once inhabited. And he preferred it that way.

But now…

"So," he said, "Sir Roderick Stafford is dead."

"Oh yes. These last two years since." Julia sunk her voice, "A suicide, I fear."

Good God! Could it be? He had met the man only once and been treated rather shabbily. Sir Roderick was an inveterate gamester, a gentleman always looking ahead toward the greater prize. And so he had with his only daughter. A second son of an earl—a mere soldier—would never have been good enough for Miss Stafford. Not when she was being courted by a baron, a viscount, and the independently wealthy third son of a marquis.

"Such a scandal, you know," Julia went on. "Miss Cavendish wrote me that most of Miss Stafford's friends cut her acquaintance. Though I do not know why she must become a governess. Surely she had relatives who might have taken her in."

Why the devil had she agreed to come here? Had she learned he was the earl now? Assumed that she might ensnare him as easily as she had before? A rush of soul-crushing bitterness surged through him. Of course she must have done. Julia had told her about the lock of hair. No doubt she believed he was still in love with her. Had assumed that he would be grateful for any crumbs of attention she scattered his way.

It would serve her right if he did marry her.

The mere thought of it stirred something deep inside of him. Something that had lain dormant for years.

Would such a bloodless marriage be so terrible? He was two and thirty. It was past time he settled down to the business of producing an heir. And Sylvia Stafford was surely as good a candidate for the next Countess of Radcliffe as any woman. Did it matter that she had cruelly shunned him once? That any interest she might have in him now was purely mercenary? It should not matter in the least. Marriage was a business transaction, nothing more. And he had wealth enough now to provide her with anything she wanted. Fine gowns, servants, even a carriage and cattle of her own if she wished it. In exchange, she would bear his children. And he would have her near. To look at. To admire. To listen to. Perhaps, in time, he might even persuade her to care for him.

Persuade her? Hell and damnation! How pathetic had he become? He stroked his thumb reflexively over the lock of hair in his hand. It would be better to send them both away. And so he would have done if Miss Stafford had not seen him. But she *had* seen him. At his very worst, too. Not only scarred and disfigured, but unshaven and in his shirtsleeves.

He recalled how carefully he had once dressed whenever he knew that he was to see her. Polished boots, pressed trousers, and an impeccably cut coat. He had always known he was not handsome, especially when compared to her other beaux, but he had never allowed himself to appear before her in less than immaculate attire.

And now, for her to have seen him like this! He clenched his fist in silent anguish. Granted, it had only been one second. Two at the most. Hardly enough time for her to have made a thorough inventory of all his faults.

But she had not screamed, he reminded himself. And she had not swooned. She had merely stood there, clutching her bonnet in her hands and staring at him.

"I daresay Miss Stafford wants to wash and change from our journey," Julia said. "And then afterward we shall take tea in the drawing room. Unless you will join us. In which case I shall have it brought to the library. It is darker there at this time of day and perhaps you will not feel so much on display." She gave him a hopeful smile. "You *will* join us, won't you Sebastian? I know Miss Stafford is simply longing to see you."

Sebastian caught Milsom looking at him with an expression of poorly disguised encouragement. He cursed bitterly. "The library, then," he growled. "In half an hour."

Chapter Three

Legs trembling beneath her, Sylvia sank down on the edge of the bed as the housekeeper withdrew from the guest chamber, shutting the door behind her. She felt breathless and ever so slightly terrified. The sight of Sebastian Conrad had shaken her to the core. He was so vastly different from in her memory. And it was not just the scars, as terrible as they were. There was something feral about him now. Something primitive and dangerous. Had war done that to him? She supposed so. Both that and excruciating physical pain.

She fully expected Lady Harker to come to her room and tell her that they were departing immediately. Before the door to Sebastian's apartments had closed, she had had a glimpse of something very like rage transforming his features. Instead, only a short time later, Lady Harker entered Sylvia's room and cheerfully informed her that Sebastian would be joining them for tea downstairs in the library in just half an hour.

"I should not have surprised him in such a way," she admitted. "He absolutely *detests* surprises and he will lose his temper. But he is not truly angry, I promise you. Indeed, he is so very pleased that you have come, Miss Stafford."

"He did not look very pleased," Sylvia said frankly.

Lady Harker gave an overbright smile. "Oh, you cannot judge my brother on his appearance. He always looks as if he is about to throttle someone." She backed toward the door. "Now I must dash if I am to be washed and changed in time for tea. But you needn't wait for me, Miss Stafford. When you are ready, go on ahead to the library. I shall meet you there directly."

Before Sylvia could think to ask where the library was located, Lady Harker was gone.

She sighed, forcing herself to rise and begin her own ablutions. Not that there was any way to adequately prepare for seeing Sebastian Conrad again after all of these years. Indeed, there was a small part of her that would rather have heard Lady Harker say that they were returning at once to London. That Sebastian had refused to see her at all.

It was not only that he had looked so alarming, both disheveled and in a scandalous state of undress. It was that in spite of his appearance—in spite of the way he had glared at her so ferociously—she had had the unreasonable urge to go to him, to cradle his face in her hands as she had done once before, and to cover him with kisses.

It had struck her then that she must still be in love with him.

It was a lowering thought. She had fought so hard to rid herself of the painful emotion. But perhaps such feelings never truly died? Or perhaps they could not be properly put to rest until she confronted him? Until she finally found out why he had abandoned her so heartlessly?

She had a suspicion, of course. Indeed, she very much feared his disappearance from her life had been her own fault.

"*The marriage mart is a sport for gentlemen,*" Penelope Mainwaring had told her three years ago. "*The more elusive the prey, the more doggedly they pursue it. But if you are one of those ridiculous females who declares herself after only one dance or who allows herself to be ravished in a closed carriage—well!—what sport is there in that? Only look at Miss Caterham's conduct last season. She told Baron Waitley that she adored him. The silly cow! Why, Waitley could not run far enough or fast enough.*"

Penelope had been her best friend since her come out and Sylvia had always endeavored to heed her advice. On this occasion, however, she had doubted. "*But surely there must be some gentlemen for whom it is not a sport,*" she had argued. "*Reticent gentlemen who desire a word or a sign from the lady they admire. Some sort of reassurance that their feelings are returned.*"

"*Try it and see,*" Penelope had warned.

Sylvia's cheeks burned to think of how spectacularly she had disregarded her former friend's advice.

But all of that was in the past, she reminded herself as she poured a ewer of water into the washbasin. She was no longer the same foolish girl who had kissed Sebastian Conrad in the Mainwaring's garden. She was a sober, levelheaded woman of the world. A woman more than capable of dealing with a little unpleasantness.

After washing and drying her hands and face, she changed into a simple, silk and woolen day dress with a narrow, white cambric collar and long, cambric-cuffed sleeves. She brushed the tangles from her thick hair, twisting it back at the nape of her neck and securing it with a handful of pins. The effect was very different from the beribboned frocks and upswept curls she had often worn in London so long ago. She looked like a governess now, she thought.

She *was* a governess.

Stiffening her spine, she left her room, making her way down the richly carpeted hall and two flights of marble stairs. A nervous housemaid directed her to the first floor library. Sylvia took a deep breath and entered.

Sebastian was there.

Alone.

He stood facing the cold fireplace, his large frame cast half in shadow. At the sound of her approach, he went unnaturally still. And then he turned around.

Sylvia clasped her hands tightly in front of her to stop their trembling.

He had shaved and combed his hair, she saw. And he was now quite properly attired in a black frock coat and trousers with a patterned waistcoat, a clean, white linen shirt, and a perfectly knotted black cravat. Except for his heavy scars and the white cast to his right eye, he looked very like the Sebastian of her memory. Tall, dark, and powerfully made. A bit intimidating, in fact.

"Miss Stafford," he said, bowing.

His voice sounded different to her ears. It was low-pitched and hoarse. And it was completely devoid of warmth. "Lord Radcliffe."

He looked at her for a long time, his expression unreadable. "Yes," he said at last. "I am Radcliffe now." He motioned to a leather-upholstered armchair near the fireplace. It was oversized and unwelcoming like everything else in the dark, cavernous room.

She crossed the short distance to it, her slow, measured steps belying the frantic beating of her heart. It was difficult to see entirely clearly. The heavy curtains were drawn and not a single gas lamp or candle burned to dispel the shadows that clung to the wood-paneled walls and carved, mahogany furnishings. But Sebastian did not seem inclined to open the curtains or to light a lamp. Quite the contrary. He appeared at home in the darkness. Or, at least, reluctant to emerge from it.

Sylvia's throat tightened with emotion, as she sat down, straightening her skirts and folding her hands primly into her lap. Sebastian took the seat across from her. He was so close that she could smell the faint, masculine scent of his shaving soap. It was spiced bergamot, she realized. The same fragrance he had favored three years before. Her already quivering stomach performed a disconcerting little somersault.

"You are well?" he asked.

"Quite well, thank you," she said. "And you…?"

His voice was cold as hoarfrost. "As you see."

Sylvia's brow creased with sympathy. *Oh, Sebastian.*

Three years ago, she would have reached out to him. She would have told him that everything was going to be all right. That it did not matter how he looked.

But now…

Now, he was a stranger. She did not know quite how to respond to him and Sebastian made no effort to put her at her ease. He merely continued to look at her in that same fathomless way.

After several moments of very strained silence, she could bear it no longer. She leaned forward in her chair, her blue eyes softly earnest, and said, "I was very sorry to hear about the death of your father and brother."

A long pause preceded his reply. "Were you?"

"Very much."

"And yet I am the earl now."

There was an underlying hint of sarcasm in his tone. She could not imagine why. She had certainly done nothing to deserve it. "A title seems poor compensation for losing two members of your family, my lord."

"A worthy sentiment."

"It is how I feel, sir. It is how *anyone* who cared about their family would feel."

He fixed her with a cold, faintly derisive stare—a stare made all the more unsettling because of his sightless eye. "Is that a reprimand, Miss Stafford?"

She had the grace to redden. "Forgive me, I did not intend—"

"Your own father is dead now, I understand."

"He is."

"A suicide, was it?"

Sylvia's polite expression slipped for an instant. It was only through sheer force of will that she was able to keep her countenance. "Yes," she said. "He shot himself two years ago. In a London gaming club, as you must know."

If she had thought to shame Sebastian with her candor, she was sorely disappointed. He betrayed not a flicker of remorse for having mentioned the scandalous death of her father. "Not the noblest course of action," he remarked.

"He had just lost everything we had on a hand of cards, my lord. I am sure he felt he had no choice."

Sebastian continued to stare at her, broodingly. "And now you are a governess."

"I am, sir."

"A rather clever governess," he continued in that same raspy, vaguely sarcastic drawl, "who has somehow managed to secure an invitation to my home."

Sylvia blinked. Good gracious! Is that what he thought? Her color heightened. "I beg your pardon, my lord, but cleverness had nothing to do with it. Lady Harker sought me out in London. She insisted I accompany her here."

"You might have refused her."

"I *did* refuse her."

"Yet, here you are."

Her eyes narrowed slightly. She did not like what he was insinuating, but she refused to rise to the bait. Lady Harker had said that Sebastian was not himself. That he was temperamental and moody. Suicidal, in fact. Is that not why Sylvia had come to Hertfordshire? To lift his spirits and help to make him well?

She was no ministering angel, not by any stretch of the imagination. And she had precious little experience handling a gentleman with the temperament of a wounded wild beast. Nevertheless, she resolved to treat him with as much kindness and courtesy as she could muster. She would even humble herself, if need be. Lord knew she had had plenty of practice at it these last two years.

"Would you prefer I go?" she asked. "I will, if that is what you wish."

Sebastian was silent for another long moment. At last, he shrugged one broad shoulder. "You are my sister's guest. Stay, by all means."

Sylvia exhaled a quiet breath. She could not help but feel like a servant who had just been granted a trial period of employment.

"No doubt it will be a welcome change from whatever it is that you do in London."

"I am a governess," she reminded him. "I teach reading, writing, drawing and music to two very young ladies."

He made a dismissive sound, indicating that this was not at all what he had meant. She waited for him to elaborate. "Whatever it is that you do when you are not teaching," he said gruffly. "Surely you do not spend every hour in the schoolroom."

"It sometimes feels like it."

"You have no time of your own?"

"Very little outside of the house."

"Even scullery maids are given a half-day on Sunday."

"So they are," Sylvia said, endeavoring not to be offended by the comparison. "But a governess is not a scullery maid, my lord. Besides which, on Sundays, I attend church with the family." She hesitated before adding, "My half-day is on Wednesday."

Sebastian absorbed this information in enigmatic silence.

"I generally do my shopping," she told him. "Or go for a walk."

His good eye was a rich, sable brown—almost black in appearance. For an instant, something flickered there. "Alone, I presume."

Sylvia had the unsettling feeling that he was asking whether or not she was presently walking out with a sweetheart. The answer was an emphatic no, but she was reluctant to own it. Least of all to the man who had rejected her. She chose her next words with care. "It is the lot of every governess to lead a solitary existence."

"Is it indeed."

"Yes. There is even a grim little pamphlet on the subject. *A Young Governess's Guide to Genteel Employment.* My father's solicitor gave it to me when I went to him for help after Papa died. It was written by a woman named Mrs. Bland, a former governess herself, I believe, and one whom I suspect was subjected to every sort of mistreatment during the course of her employment." She gave a wholly unconscious smile. "I have often since considered writing an advice pamphlet of my own. Something a bit more hopeful. Though I daresay it would not sell half as well. Mrs. Bland had a distinct turn for the Gothic."

Sebastian did not appear to be amused by her attempt at a lighthearted story. Indeed, he was looking at her just as haughtily as he had since she first entered the room. "You will forgive me, Miss Stafford, but I find it hard to believe that you are perfectly content as some manner of superior servant."

Sylvia's smile faded slowly. His words stung. Perhaps he had meant them to. Or perhaps, he genuinely could not fathom a person finding happiness after so much adversity?

"No," she said. "I cannot claim perfect contentment, my lord. I do not know many who can. But I am a good deal more content than I was in the months following Papa's death. Those were very bleak days indeed. I might have been overwhelmed with grief if

I had not had to immediately seek my living. In any case, I soon discovered that melancholy was no match for industry. The busier I kept myself, the easier it all became. And now, though I'm not perfectly content by any means, I can say that yes, I am happy in my new situation."

"Your new situation being a merchant's house in Cheapside." He made no effort to hide his disdain. "Tell me, Miss Stafford, did the scandal of your father's death prevent you from finding employment with people of quality?"

"People of quality?" she repeated, astonished. The Sebastian she remembered would never have used such a phrase. Had he become so toplofty now that he was the earl? Or was this yet another attempt to put her in her place? "As opposed to Mr. and Mrs. Dinwiddy, do you mean?"

He gave a curt nod.

"I don't know, really," she admitted. "I did not attempt to find employment amongst my former acquaintance."

"Too proud?"

"Yes. Perhaps a little. But it was not only my pride. To own the truth, I can imagine nothing more uncomfortable for my former friends than having me in their home as a paid employee. Not that they would ever have considered hiring me. I'm accomplished enough to instruct the daughters of a merchant, but I doubt there are many parents of what you call the quality who would find my limited talents acceptable. And then there is the matter of Papa's death…"

"After which, all of your friends deserted you."

"That's right."

"And all of your suitors, too, I imagine."

That startled her. "Suitors? What suitors? Do you mean…" She was sorely tempted to laugh. "Surely you do not intend to blame *your* behavior on my father's unfortunate actions?"

Sebastian frowned. "*My* behavior?"

"If so, I suggest you reconsider the timing. You were in India nearly a year before my father took his own life. *Nearly a year*, my lord."

She would not have thought his gaze could grow any colder, but at the look he now gave her, Sylvia was astonished that she did not instantly transform into an icicle.

"I am well aware of the time I spent in India, madam," he said with awful civility. "Every minute of it. But what my service there can have to do with either you or your father is, I confess, a mystery to me."

She flushed. "You willfully misunderstand me, sir. It has nothing to do with your service and everything to do with—"

"Oh dear! Is it half past already?" Lady Harker's cheerful voice rang out from the doorway, bringing an abrupt and altogether merciful end to their conversation. "How thoroughly vexing," she said, "when I made such an effort to be punctual!"

Sebastian glowered at his sister. He knew very well that she had contrived to leave him alone with Miss Stafford. He suspected that Miss Stafford knew it too. And if her expression of relief was any indication, she had no more interest in renewing their relationship than he did.

"I do hope you are hungry, Miss Stafford." Julia entered the room, the servants close behind. "Though how you could not be, I do not know, for you scarcely touched your food at the inn." She turned to address a footman. "Put the tea tray there, Thomas." She gestured to the cluster of furniture near the fireplace. "Yes, that's right. I shall ring if we need anything else."

Sebastian had risen at his sister's arrival, but now resumed his seat. "You dined at a coaching inn?"

"I would hardly call it dining," Julia said. She fluffed her voluminous skirts out around her as she settled into her chair. "The man at the Bull could offer us no more than a cold pasty and some warm ale."

"*The Bull*?" His temper flared. "What in blazes were you thinking to stop at such a place?"

"That we were hungry," Julia said, adding candidly, "and we needed to use the necessary."

The color rose in Miss Stafford's cheeks at Julia's indelicate reply. "Your sister was in no danger, my lord," she said. "I engaged a private parlor for us and we stayed only long enough for the coachman to tend to the horses."

"There, you see." Julia occupied herself with pouring out their tea. "We were perfectly safe." As she filled Sebastian's cup, she glanced up at him, her lips parting as if to speak. He returned her gaze, silently daring her to mention his inability to drink in company. After a heavily weighted moment, Julia's mouth closed again and she handed him his teacup.

"Why in God's name didn't you take the train?" he asked.

Julia shrugged. "Harker does not like it. Not after the derailment at Tottenham station in February."

Sebastian frowned. The derailment had claimed the lives of five passengers and two of the railway men. He could well imagine Harker forbidding his wife from train travel in the aftermath. Though how his brother-in-law thought that it was any safer for Julia to be careening around the countryside in a coach and four, Sebastian had no idea.

"The Bull is suitable for changing out your horses and nothing more," he said. "The Inn itself is far from respectable. No lady should ever cross its threshold." He cast a stony glance at Miss Stafford. "Not even a governess."

Miss Stafford returned his gaze, her blue eyes flashing briefly with something very like indignation. Something very like hurt. It was gone before he could decipher it, her expression once again reverting into lines of polite indifference.

What he wouldn't give to see her rattled! She had almost lost her composure in the seconds before Julia's arrival. A few moments longer and she might have dropped this infuriating mask of civility. She might have shouted at him. Slapped him. He had certainly given her ample reason. "I will instruct the coachman not to stop there on your return to Cheapside," he said.

"There is no need, my lord," she replied. "I shall be quite happy to take the train."

Sebastian affected not to care, even as his brain conjured images of Miss Stafford, alone and vulnerable, in a crowded railway car. "As you wish."

Julia paused in the midst of slicing a piece of plum cake to scowl at him. "Miss Stafford is not returning to London for a month, at least. There is no reason for us to be discussing her journey back." She turned to Miss Stafford, proffering the piece of cake on a small, painted porcelain plate. "He's concerned for your safety, that's all. Not that he will ever admit it."

Sebastian's jaw hardened. He said nothing. What was there to say? Of course he was concerned for her safety. What gentleman wouldn't be? She was an unmarried woman with neither family nor fortune.

A beautiful unmarried woman.

He looked at her now, just as he had looked at her when she appeared outside his rooms. He could not seem to stop looking at her. She was sitting primly on the edge of her chair, doing nothing more than drinking her tea and listening to Julia. Gone were the fashionable gowns, the delicate satin slippers, and the sapphire clips that had once held up her lustrous chestnut hair. In their place was the drab costume of a governess.

Next to Julia, bedecked in her ribbons, ruffles, and that godawful wire crinoline, Miss Stafford's clothing looked positively second-rate. Her dress was plain to the point of being severe, her wide skirts falling without a single flounce and her bodice lacking any trimming other than a row of very serviceable buttons which marched from her slender waist straight up to the ivory column of her throat.

But it had never been about her finery. With or without rich fabrics and jewels, Sylvia Stafford still managed to shine like a diamond. She was lovelier now than in his memory—a fact which he would not have thought possible. And yet, one glimpse of her dimpled smile had nearly stopped his heart. And the sound of her voice…

That soft, velvet voice.

Three years ago, it had had the power to enthrall him. To bring him to his knees. And when she had walked into the library, when she had addressed him as Lord Radcliffe for the first time, he had realized that, if he was not careful, there was a very real danger it would do so again. The knowledge had only increased his bitterness toward her.

"Besides," Julia continued, "when you return home, Harker and I will accompany you. And perhaps my brother…" She cast another meaningful glance in his direction. "But it is too soon to speak of that. Better we should talk about all the amusements I have planned for us here at Pershing."

"Amusements?" Miss Stafford looked genuinely alarmed at the prospect. "I do hope you have not gone to any trouble on my account, Lady Harker."

"And why shouldn't I? You are my guest. I would host a ball if Sebastian would allow it. But no. We shall have to content ourselves with country amusements.

You once spent a good deal of time in the country, did you not, Miss Stafford? Before your father…That is to say, before all the unpleasantness?"

"Yes. I grew up at Newell Park. I was there until I made my come out."

"Newell Park?"

"The principal seat of the Stafford baronets in Kent. It's occupied by the present baronet now. Sir George. He is a very distant cousin of my father."

Julia wrinkled her nose. "I do believe I've met him. It was last summer in London. At a party given by Lord and Lady Graves. It was an awful crush—" She broke off. "But that is neither here nor there. We were speaking of the countryside and country amusements. I expect you can ride, Miss Stafford?"

"Yes, of course."

Julia took a bite of cake. "I keep one of my own favorite mares here year round. Regrettably, I know absolutely nothing about the other horses in the stable. Most of them were bought by my brother, Edmund, before he died. But no matter. I daresay Sebastian will be able to choose a satisfactory mount for you."

He saw Miss Stafford's blue gaze flicker to his. She was embarrassed by his sister's presumption, that much he could tell. But there was something else, too. Something in her eyes that he could not interpret. "How long has it been since you have ridden, Miss Stafford?" he asked.

"Two years, my lord."

Since her father had died, then. No doubt her horse had been among the items lost in that final hand of cards. "If you are out of practice, you would do well on Ares. He is safe enough for a rider of moderate skill without being dead on all four legs."

Miss Stafford's eyes met his briefly. She did not appear at all offended by his unjust characterization of her competence in the saddle. Quite the opposite, in fact. She seemed to believe him. "I hope I *am* still a rider of moderate skill."

"One does not forget how to ride, Miss Stafford."

"No, I suppose not. But it *has* been a very long time. I do not even have a riding costume anymore."

"You shall wear one of mine," said Julia. "And I know just the one, too. It is dark blue and has the most divine little jacket with mousquetaire cuffs. The very latest style. My maid, Craddock, can make any adjustments necessary. She is a dab hand with a needle and thread."

"It is kind of you to offer, Lady Harker, but you needn't lend me anything half so fine."

Sebastian regarded Miss Stafford from beneath lowered brows. Had she always been so excruciatingly polite? So damnably respectful? It grated on him. To think that the proud, vibrant creature he had known three years ago in London was reduced to such a state. It made him feel...almost guilty. But why should it? He was not responsible for her change in station. She had her father to blame for that. And herself, too. For if she had married him three years ago, she would be a countess now. Instead she had treated him appallingly. Rejecting him without so much as a by your leave.

To say that she had broken his heart was maudlin romantic nonsense—besides being an understatement. Good God, her rejection had practically unmanned him! She was the first and only woman he had ever loved. And now she was here. Revealing herself as no better than the mercenary, grasping females who had once pursued his titled elder brother. Even worse, she was acting as if they had never been anything more to each other than the barest acquaintances. As if he had never held her in his arms. As if she had never touched him and kissed him.

Unless her mysterious remark about *his behavior* was some allusion to that night in the Mainwaring's garden.

Could that be her game? To use his conduct of three years ago as some sort of leverage to wring a proposal out of him? His fingers tightened reflexively on the handle of his teacup, the hot liquid sloshing dangerously against the brim. He had always considered himself a good judge of character. As a soldier, he had had to be. And yet somehow, three years ago, he had managed to misjudge Sylvia Stafford completely.

Oblivious to his escalating temper, Julia chattered on, telling Miss Stafford about the shops in the nearby village of Apsley Heath and opining on her favorite places to walk and to ride. She even launched into a brief—and wholly inaccurate—treatise on the history of Pershing Hall itself.

Miss Stafford was not so blind to his mood as his sister. More than once he saw her glance in his direction, her face pale and her slim hands unsteady on her teacup. She had never been scared of him in the past, despite the fact that he towered over her and outweighed her by several stone. Was it the sight of his scars that unsettled her now? He knew they were repellant, but were they so monstrous that they genuinely frightened her?

And if this was her reaction in the shadowy gloom of the library, what might she make of his ravaged face in the full light of day?

A helpless fury stirred within him. He did not love her anymore. Indeed, he often felt as if he hated her. Even so, he could not bear the thought of her recoiling from him in horror.

He looked at her sitting across from him now, so dainty and perfect and beautiful, and he cursed Julia for bringing her here. He cursed himself, too, for having kept that damned lock of her hair.

"Are you an early riser in the country, Miss Stafford?" Julia was asking. "For if you are, I would have us ride before breakfast."

"Yes. If you like."

"Splendid," Julia said brightly. "Naturally, you will want to become acquainted with your mount. Though, we needn't wait until the morning for that. We can all go down to the stables after tea and—"

"No," Miss Stafford said, interrupting before he could voice an objection himself. She lowered her teacup into her saucer. "I am obliged to you, Lady Harker, but I think...If you do not mind it...I would rather rest in my room for a while. I'm a bit tired from our journey."

"Oh! How silly of me. Of course, you are. Shall I accompany you upstairs or—"

Miss Stafford rose. "No. Please don't disturb yourself on my account. I shall see myself up."

Sebastian stood, watching her intently. She was distracted. Upset. He brutally suppressed another frisson of guilt. "Is there anything you require?" he asked.

"No, sir. Nothing." She addressed herself to his cravat, clearly unable to bring herself to look at his ruin of a face.

"I'll send my maid to wake you before dinner," Julia said.

"Thank you, my lady. My lord. I bid you both good afternoon."

Sebastian remained standing until she had gone from the room. Only then did he resume his seat, his expression shuttered.

"What did you say to her before I arrived?" Julia demanded.

"Nothing."

"Nothing? She looked as if she was about to cry. And she hardly said two words during tea." Julia's own eyes puddled in sympathy. "I worked so hard to find her and bring her here for you, Sebastian. And now you will ruin it with your temper. Just because you may threaten to wring my neck does not mean you may do so to Miss Stafford."

"I did not threaten to wring Miss Stafford's neck," he growled.

"Well, whatever you said, I wouldn't be at all surprised to find her packing her things at this very moment!"

Sebastian's stomach clenched in alarm.

"I shall have to go to her and tell her…Oh, but what *can* I tell her? That you're pleased she's here? That you wish her to stay? I know you must do, Sebastian, for you couldn't stop staring at her all through tea. If you would only say something kind to her—"

"The devil!" he swore under his breath. Was this to be a repeat of three years ago? Was he to humiliate himself? To beg and plead with Sylvia Stafford for some small crumb of her affection? He glared at his sister. "You are the one who invited her here."

"Yes, but—"

"If you wish her to remain, then you must persuade her."

"But I only did it for you! Because of that lock of hair. I knew you would wish to see her. And I knew—"

"You know nothing about it," he said harshly. "I'll not permit you to interfere with my life, Julia. Do you understand me?"

Julia's bottom lip wobbled, but though she gave every appearance of being on the verge of a tearful display, Sebastian could not help but notice the stubborn set of her chin. It was a feature that was distinctly Conrad. "It is not interference," she informed him, "if I have done it for your own good."

Chapter Four

Miss Craddock, Lady Harker's personal maid, arrived at dawn with the altered riding costume draped over her arm. She was a stern woman of middle-years who brooked no nonsense and, before Sylvia could utter more than a cursory protest, she had assisted her into the dark blue habit, skillfully arranged her hair, and was pinning into place a very fashionable riding hat.

Sylvia was ashamed at how easily she fell back into the role of privileged, pampered young lady. Over and over again, she reminded herself that she was no longer a member of the society to which she had been born. That she was a governess of absolutely no consequence. A superior servant, as Sebastian had said so unkindly. She had no business sitting at a dressing table, allowing Craddock to brush her hair. And she had no right to don the stylish riding costume lent to her by Lady Harker.

She reminded herself how hard it had been to adjust to her new life in Cheapside after her father's death. She had had to learn to be independent. To see to her own needs. There had been no one to help her dress or to arrange her hair at the Dinwiddy's. No one to press her gowns or mend a torn hem. It was up to her to see that her clothing remained clean and in good order. And it was up to her to arrange her hair as quickly and efficiently as possible each morning before beginning lessons in the schoolroom.

She stood in front of the gilt framed looking glass, scarcely able to credit the transformation that Craddock had wrought in so short a time. She was taller than Lady Harker, as well as being slimmer in the waist and fuller in the bosom, but the skillful lady's maid had managed to lengthen the voluminous skirts, take in the waist of the riding jacket, and somehow add an extra inch to the elaborately cuffed sleeves. Worn over a starched petticoat and muslin chemisette, the dark blue habit now fit her body as if it had been made for her.

If that were not enough to render her speechless, her hair—which she had grown so used to seeing in a simple chignon or coil of braids—was now prettily rolled into the confines of a fine, silk hair net. When combined with the little riding hat perched atop her head and the borrowed riding costume gracefully skimming the curves of her figure, she no longer bore any resemblance to Sylvia Stafford, governess. Instead, the image reflected back at her in the mirror was that of the glorious Miss Stafford of Newell Park. A lady that Sylvia did not know anymore. A stranger.

She frowned at her reflection.

"You're unhappy with it, miss?" Craddock asked as she handed her a pair of Lady Harker's worsted riding gloves.

"Not at all." Sylvia made an effort to smile. "I like it very much. Indeed, I believe you have worked a minor miracle."

"I've only done what milady bid me."

"You have done it exceedingly well." Sylvia tugged on her borrowed gloves. They were uncommonly snug. "Is Lady Harker waiting at the stables?"

"I expect so, miss." Craddock collected her sewing basket. "Will you be needing anything else?"

"No. Thank you, Craddock."

Craddock dropped a perfunctory curtsy and left the room. Sylvia wondered what the lady's maid thought of her. The entire staff must know by now that she was a governess in a merchant's household. And when it came to distinctions of rank and wealth, servants could be even more toplofty than their employers. How long would it be before the butler or the housekeeper made some subtle attempt to depress her pretensions?

As if she could have any pretensions after that disastrous meeting with Sebastian!

He had been distant and cold, making it abundantly clear that she was not of his class. Indeed, at times, she could almost have sworn that he hated her.

It puzzled her exceedingly. She knew she had been foolish. And he had a right to be wary of her after what she had done. But to hate her for it? She could not understand it.

Exiting her room, she made her way down the curving, marble staircase. Yesterday, she had been too tired and overwhelmed to appreciate her surroundings. Today, it was difficult to refrain from looking all about her.

She was no stranger to grand houses. Newell Park had often been called a Palladian jewel box and the Mainwaring's familial estate in Devon could easily have doubled for a medieval castle. Pershing Hall, however, was something else altogether. It had the requisite paintings and pillars, of course, and the main hall itself was possessed of a truly spectacular domed ceiling. But it was a sprawling, illogical structure. Built in competing architectural styles, it appeared to Sylvia that every generation had added something new. A Tudor arch, Elizabethan chimneys, and Palladian columns. She could not even begin to fathom how many rooms it must have or how long it would take to walk from one end of the house to the other.

To think that Sebastian lived here, all alone except for his servants and the occasional visits from his sister! It was a sobering thought.

And yet, Sebastian Conrad had never been the sort of gentleman who enjoyed society. He had been quiet and aloof, his severe gaze hinting at disapproval as it drifted over the various gaieties of the season.

"*I do not know why he bothers to come!*" Penelope Mainwaring had complained once during a musical evening at Lord and Lady Lovejoy's townhouse in Mayfair.

Sylvia had consented to sing two songs that night. Sebastian had been at the back of the room. She had felt his eyes on her throughout her brief performance. It was early in their courtship then—if it could even be called a courtship. She had not known quite what to make of him yet. But somehow, even then, his solemn, steady regard made the practiced flirtations of her other beaux seem childish and silly.

He had been so much more imposing than other gentlemen. So much more serious. He had not given her effusive compliments or made a show of teasing her. He had just been there. Formidable. Reliable. Trustworthy. And because he had not appeared to give his affections easily, she had valued his attention all the more.

Of course, that had only been at the beginning. Later, when she had spent more time with him, talked to him and got to know him, she had come to care for him deeply.

Not that any of that mattered anymore.

They were two different people now. Virtual strangers who were not even inclined to like each other very much.

She descended the final flight of stairs, so lost in her own thoughts that she did not see the servant bounding up the steps from below. He was carrying a can of hot water and an armful of folded towels. At the sight of her, he stopped short. Water sloshed over the edge of the wide spout and splashed onto the steps.

"Oh, I do beg your pardon!" she said. "I didn't mean to startle you."

"No indeed, miss. It was my own fault."

"Nonsense." She stepped down to where he stood. "If you can spare a towel?"

"A towel?"

She cast a pointed glance to the small puddle at his feet. "I would hate for someone to slip on the stairs."

"You needn't trouble yourself. I'll tend to it myself when—"

"No trouble at all. I'll make short work of it." She took the topmost towel from the stack in his arms and, in one smooth movement, knelt down and mopped up the spill. "There, you see?" She rose to find him regarding her with a slightly furrowed brow and an assessing glint in his sharp, foxlike eyes.

Her smile faded. She had the uncomfortable feeling that her relative value was being weighed and measured down to the inch. "Forgive me," she said, "but are you his lordship's valet?"

"I have that honor, miss."

She slowly folded the damp towel. She had wondered if Sebastian would be joining them for their ride this morning. But if his valet was only now bringing up his shaving things, he clearly had no intention of doing so. "Well..." She extended the folded towel. "I'll not keep you then."

"Thank you, miss." He gave her as much of a bow as he could manage with his arms full.

She watched him for a moment as he continued his ascent up the stairs. He had been Sebastian's batman, had he not? More than anyone else, he must know about Sebastian's state of mind. She was terribly tempted to question him, but something in the way he had looked at her convinced her to hold her tongue. She could not be entirely certain, but she had the distinct impression that Milsom would never divulge any of his master's secrets—least of all to her.

Sebastian tilted his head back, allowing Milsom to run a shaving razor up the length of his throat with a practiced flick. "You're damnably quiet this morning," he grumbled.

"Am I, my lord?"

"Not conspiring with my sister again, are you?"

Milsom lowered his brows in disapproval. "I should think not, sir." He made another pass with the razor. "I never did *conspire* with anyone."

"No? What would you call it, then?"

"Can't say what I'd call it." Milsom considered for a moment. "Her ladyship plagued me about that lock of hair of yours until I confessed the name of the female who gave it to you." He swiped the razor along the edge of Sebastian's jaw. "Don't expect anyone could withstand her ladyship once she's got an idea in her head."

Sebastian frowned. "Perhaps not."

"I resisted her as long as I was able."

"That bad, was it?"

"You've no idea, my lord." Milsom grimaced at the memory.

"She cried, I suppose."

"A great deal, sir."

Sebastian was not wholly unsympathetic. He knew from bitter experience that Julia could make a damned nuisance of herself if she did not get her way. Still, he had thought his valet was made of sterner stuff. "The trouble with you, Milsom, is that you haven't the first idea how to defend yourself against feminine wiles."

"Don't reckon I do, my lord." Milsom stood back to assess his handiwork. "There's never been much cause to learn, has there?" Seemingly satisfied with the quality of his master's shave, he turned to the dressing table and busied himself with cleaning up. "Speaking of the fairer sex…I saw your Miss Stafford this morning."

Sebastian's traitorous heart gave a painful lurch. He scowled. "She's not *my* Miss Stafford, Milsom."

"She was dressed up to ride with her ladyship."

"Was she?" Sebastian rose and went to the washstand. He was up and dressed himself, but not because he intended to join them. Indeed, riding out onto the estate, exposing his scarred face to the unforgiving morning sunlight, was the very last thing he wished to do.

Besides, he thought as he splashed his face with cold water and dried it roughly with a towel, he had no interest in renewing his relationship with Miss Stafford.

"She was looking uncommonly handsome, if I may say so," Milsom remarked from his place at the dressing table.

Sebastian shot his valet a ferocious glare. "No, Milsom. You may *not* say so."

Milsom shrugged. "Might be that Miss Stafford and her ladyship haven't rode out yet. I expect you could still join them if—"

"Damn your impertinence," Sebastian growled. "It's bad enough I must hear this sort of thing from my sister. I'll not countenance it from you."

"As you say, my lord. But seeing as how you're the Earl of Radcliffe now—"

"Milsom—"

"And you'll be needing a countess." Milsom coughed discreetly. "And an heir."

Sebastian raked a hand through his hair. "A countess and an heir," he muttered. "Hell and damnation."

He strode out of his bedchamber and through the doors that led to his private sitting room. It was a thoroughly masculine space, with an enormous desk of polished mahogany, a stuffed sofa and chairs, and dark, heavy wood tables adorned with glass oil lamps, inlaid boxes, and a smattering of Far Eastern objet d'art that had been collected by his father many years before.

It was where he did most of his reading and his writing now. It was also where Milsom brought his meals. He rarely saw the rest of the staff at Pershing and, except for the occasional foray into the library or the even rarer twilight gallop over the grounds, he did not often stray from his apartments. It was isolating, yes, but far from uncomfortable. Especially when compared with the accommodations he had endured in India.

But then, the Earl of Radcliffe's apartments were large and luxurious by any measure. Along with the rest of the family quarters, they occupied a great portion of the west wing and connected, via adjoining dressing rooms, to the equally impressive apartments of the Countess of Radcliffe—apartments that had stood vacant since the death of his mother two decades before.

Apartments that, if he married, would house his own countess.

He cursed Milsom for bringing up such a thing. Not that the thought had been far from his mind since Miss Stafford's arrival.

That first year after returning to India, he had lived on dreams of her. Dreams of holding her. Kissing her. Marrying her. Those dreams had suffered a particularly painful death, but now… to think that Sylvia Stafford was once again within his reach.

He had the wealth and the title now. And he could have her, too, if he wanted her. Perhaps not in the way he had once imagined. Not as his beloved, nor even as his friend. But what difference did sentiment make? If he wed her, she would do her duty by him and consider it a small price to pay for the privilege of having been made the Countess of Radcliffe.

The thought gave Sebastian little comfort.

Restless and irritable, he prowled the length of the room, only to stop, quite abruptly, at one of the velvet-draped windows that faced the park. Tension coiled in his stomach. Everything within him warned that he must stay on his guard. That he mustn't give in to curiosity. Or to longing.

Naturally, such sensible internal advice had no effect at all.

Leaning his shoulder against the window frame, he folded his arms across his chest and stared, broodingly, out across the grounds toward the imposing stone outbuildings that made up the Pershing Hall stables.

There was no sign of Miss Stafford and his sister, but unless he was very much mistaken in her character, Julia would make a point of guiding her guest down the one riding path of which the bank of windows in the Earl of Radcliffe's apartments had an unobstructed view.

He was not mistaken.

Only a short time later, he caught his first glimpse of two horses weaving along the narrow bridle path in the distance. The riders were too far away to make out just yet, but he recognized his sister's dappled gray mare, and the gleaming, dark copper coat of Ares, the bay gelding that he had recommended for Miss Stafford.

He waited impatiently for the two women to come into view. It did not take long. There was a cluster of trees which briefly blocked the path, a glare from the sun which temporarily obstructed his vision. And then, suddenly, there they were.

There *she* was.

He exhaled slowly.

She was perched atop Ares' back, wearing a dark blue riding costume that appeared to be molded to her every curve. Her cheeks were flushed from exercise, her expression oddly grave under the brim of a dashing little hat. Ares danced sideways on the path, seeming to take exception to the wind as it rustled the branches in an overhanging tree, but Miss Stafford handled him expertly. She had an impeccable seat. And, even from a distance, he could appreciate how soft her gloved hands were on the reins.

She had always been an excellent horsewoman. He had observed as much in London on the few occasions he had managed to "accidentally" cross her path when she was out for her morning ride in Hyde Park. She had ridden a bay gelding then, too. Sebastian remembered how, in the bright sunlight, the highlights in her hair had gleamed to match its coat.

He shifted where he stood, settling his shoulder more firmly against the window frame as he watched Miss Stafford urge Ares forward to ride abreast with the dappled mare. She said something to Julia—he wished he knew what it was—and then she leaned forward in her saddle and stroked Ares gently on the neck.

God, but the sight of her made him ache. As much now as it had three years ago. A painful, physical ache that he could feel in every corner of his being.

It made him uneasy, too. Even more so than it had done when she first arrived. He could not think why. Unless it had something to do with the way she was dressed. The fashionable, blue habit she had on was startlingly different from the drab, shapeless gown she had worn yesterday.

And he *was* startled.

She no longer looked like a governess, he realized. She looked instead very much as she had once looked in London.

Yet something about Sylvia Stafford was profoundly different. He could not quite put his finger on it. Perhaps it was simply his own altered view of her after having been jilted so heartlessly. Perhaps, after three long years, he was at last seeing her as she really was. A faithless flirt. A fortune hunter. A woman who, when it came down to it, likely had no more sense of honor than her dissolute father had had before her.

He wanted to hate her. At the same time, much to his mortification, he wanted to grab hold of her, to pull her into his arms and cover her soft mouth with his.

The very idea of it was laughable.

As disfigured as he was, how could he ever presume to touch her? She would recoil in horror. She would swoon or run away screaming. Not that he could imagine Miss Stafford doing any of those things. She had always seemed to have more than her fair share of courage. Even so, she was not an automaton. She was a flesh and blood woman. She would not be able to disguise her revulsion. He would see it in her face the moment he attempted to touch her.

Sebastian turned away from the window in disgust. Why the devil was he even considering any of this? He was not going to marry Miss Stafford. She was not going to be his countess. Milsom and Julia's suggestion was a ridiculous fantasy, not worthy of a first thought, let alone a second.

Besides, he thought bitterly as he sat down at his desk, how the devil did they expect him to convince Miss Stafford to marry him? And even if he could—even if she *was* as mercenary as he suspected—what in blazes did they think would happen next? That she would miraculously cease to be horrified by his scarred face? That she would willingly allow him to kiss her? To bed her? It was pure madness. If he had an ounce of sense, he would put it directly out of his mind.

He uncapped the inkwell and ruthlessly dipped the steel nib of his pen into the black fluid within. He had a paper to write for a new philosophical journal in Edinburgh. There were books to read. Notes to organize. More than enough work to keep him busy for the rest of the day and into the evening, too. He had wasted enough time brooding over Sylvia Stafford. He resolved to think on her no more.

It was a resolution that lasted only as long as the next morning.

Chapter Five

After three days at Pershing Hall with no sign of Sebastian, Sylvia came to a decision. She informed Lady Harker of it that evening at dinner after the liveried footman who had served their first course had withdrawn. The two of them were left alone, seated with relative intimacy at one end of the long, polished mahogany table that dominated Pershing Hall's cavernous dining room. "I do think it would be best," she said.

Lady Harker regarded her with an expression of bewilderment. "But I still don't understand, Miss Stafford. Is it because of *me*? Is it something I have done? I know I have been rather managing, but—"

"It is not that."

"Then why must you consider returning to London so soon? Are you not enjoying your stay here?"

Sylvia sighed. She *was* enjoying her stay. A little too much, in fact. There were no balls or parties at Pershing Hall, of course, and no visits to the neighboring estates, but every morning she had gone riding with Lady Harker, mounted on the most divine bay gelding she had ever had the privilege to ride. She had breakfasted in bed, spent quiet evenings stitching at an embroidery frame in the drawing room, and even taken a long, hot bath in a full-sized tub.

It was luxury of the sort she had not experienced in years. She would have had to be made of stone not to appreciate it. But she had not come to Pershing Hall to please herself. She had come to help Sebastian.

"I am having a wonderful time," she said. "But I have been here three days and I have only seen Lord Radcliffe once."

Lady Harker's soupspoon paused in the air midway between her bowl and her mouth. "Is *that* all that's troubling you?" She laughed. "Three days is nothing, Miss Stafford. Why, it is not uncommon for my brother to avoid me for an entire visit. If I did not seek him out in his apartments, I daresay I would not see him at all."

"But you are his sister, ma'am. I am only a houseguest. And a female one at that. I can hardly disturb him in his rooms."

"Naturally not. It would be most improper." Lady Harker swallowed her spoonful of soup. "I shall have to contrive a way to lure him out."

Sylvia considered this as she applied herself to her own soup. It was a rich, creamy asparagus that had been cooked to perfection. Another luxury, she thought grimly. It really would not do to become used to such things.

"Lady Harker," she attempted again, "if Lord Radcliffe truly does not wish to see me, then perhaps it *would* be best for me to return to London. I honestly don't see how I can be of any help if I remain. My arrival seems to have done nothing but aggravate him and, if you are concerned for his state of mind, surely it would not do to upset him further."

"He is always aggravated. Indeed, I do not believe he has spoken a civil word to me since his return from India." Lady Harker laughed once more. The sound was a trifle strained. "My brother Edmund was used to say that Sebastian had spent too many years at war. That he had forgotten how to talk to civilized people and knew only how to order other soldiers about. But I think he must not have been so uncivil to you, Miss Stafford."

Sylvia smiled dryly. "He was quite uncivil to me when I arrived here."

"Not then." Lady Harker gave a dismissive wave of her hand. "Though I do wish he had behaved better. Indeed, I *thought* he would. Why else would he have agreed to come downstairs and join us? He *never* comes downstairs when I am staying at Pershing. I hoped he would have…"

Sylvia raised her brows in polite enquiry. "Would have what?"

"I don't know, really." Lady Harker frowned. "But I thought he would do *something*." She fingered the stem of her wineglass. "What was he like when you knew him before?"

Sylvia felt a distinct pang of sadness. She ignored it. It was not the first time since her arrival she had been struck with melancholy. She supposed it was only natural given the circumstances. "Oh…He was much the same, if I recall."

"The same as he is *now*?" Lady Harker was aghast. "Surely not!"

"Well, perhaps he was a bit kinder then," Sylvia conceded. She did not expound on the subject. Lady Harker was pleasant company and had made her very welcome at Pershing Hall, but she was a talebearer, however well intentioned, and the last thing Sylvia wanted was to have her thoughts and feelings about the Earl of Radcliffe bandied about the fashionable world.

"I cannot think what you saw in him," Lady Harker said. "Unless…Was he in uniform when first you met him?"

Sylvia's mouth lifted in a bemused half-smile. "I believe he was. Yes."

"Ah, that explains it. Lucinda Cavendish says that no lady can resist a man in uniform, try as she might. And if the gentleman is a cavalry officer, so much the worse!"

Lady Harker finished her soup, laying her spoon down beside her empty bowl. Almost immediately two footmen entered the dining room. They removed the asparagus soup with *vol-au-vents* of chicken, lamb cutlets with cucumbers, and side dishes of spinach, broccoli, and stewed mushrooms.

Sylvia helped herself to a little of each, wondering how in the world she was going to resign herself to the simple fare that she dined on at the Dinwiddy's after having enjoyed so much rich cuisine at Pershing Hall. She very much feared that when she returned to Cheapside she would experience once again the feelings of gloom and discontent which had so plagued her when she had first entered service two years before.

She was accustomed to it now, of course. But when she had arrived at the Dinwiddy's, still dressed in black after the death of her father, the period of adjustment had been difficult indeed. The small attic bedroom to which the housekeeper, Mrs. Poole, had consigned her had been quite a shock after her luxurious rooms at Newell Park. So too had been the slice of cold mutton pie which had comprised her dinner that first evening. The Dinwiddy's were very kind—she was the first to admit it—but that kindness did not extend to offering their governess the choice cuts of meat. And it certainly did not allow for housing her in one of their best bedrooms.

"Will you work on your embroidery again after dinner, Miss Stafford?" Lady Harker asked.

Sylvia dabbed her mouth with her napkin. "Yes, I think so. Unless you have something else you would like me to do?"

"No, no, I have promised a letter to Harker. It is really quite tedious. I do so loathe writing letters." She raised her wine glass to her lips. "You will want to write to your friends as well. When you do, you must give your letters to me and I will have Craddock post them along with mine."

"I am obliged to you, but it is not necessary."

"Not necessary? Why ever not?"

"I have no one with whom I correspond anymore."

Lady Harker's eyes filled with sudden sympathy. "Oh, don't you?"

Sylvia felt again that same twinge of sadness. This time, it was not so easy to dismiss. "It is of little matter," she said, forcing another smile. "I much prefer to work at the embroidery frame while I can. If I am very industrious, I may even complete the pattern that you gave me before I return to London."

This seemed to placate Lady Harker—and to distract her, too. She instantly went off into rhapsodies about the lovely pattern she had found in an issue of the *Ladies' Treasury* several months before. By the time she paused to draw breath, she seemed to have forgotten Sylvia's pathetic situation entirely.

Sylvia believed herself to have forgotten it, too. It was only later, after several hours spent in the drawing room, stitching in silence while Lady Harker attended to her correspondence, that she began to feel the full effects of her unhappiness. She excused herself to bed and, as she climbed the sweeping staircase, a single beeswax candle lighting her way, she remembered how it had felt to do the same at Newell Park.

Her shoulders slumped beneath the weight of her silk dinner dress. She was cold and tired. She wanted to go home. Not to Cheapside. Not to her attic room at the Dinwiddy's. She wanted to go *home*. She wanted to wake up tomorrow in her familiar bed with its familiar rose silk hangings and discover that the last two years had all been nothing but a terrible dream. And as for Papa…

She swallowed back a sudden swell of tears.

Papa was gone forever.

She had no one but herself now.

Which was exactly why it would not do to indulge in an episode of hysterics, she told herself firmly. She dashed away a tear that trickled down her cheek, straightened her spine, and proceeded down the dark corridor to her room.

Too late she heard the creak of a floorboard and felt the subtle shift in the atmosphere that could only be caused by the presence of another person. She raised her candle higher. The flame flickered wildly. "Is someone there?"

Sebastian stepped out of the darkness.

Sylvia caught her breath. "Oh," she whispered. "It's you."

He loomed over her, his black hair disheveled and his cravat untied. He did not look happy to see her. Indeed, he looked as grim and forbidding as ever. But in her present state of mind, he was the dearest sight in the whole world. Her heart gave a mad leap and, for several weighted seconds, it was all she could do not to fling herself into his arms and weep out all of her troubles against one of his broad shoulders.

"Are you lost, Miss Stafford?" he asked.

"No, my lord."

"You have been standing here for some time."

"Have I?" She lowered her candle, mortified to think that he had been observing her. "I beg your pardon. I didn't realize—" She flushed. "I was wool-gathering, I'm afraid."

"Were you indeed."

"Yes, I...I am on my way to bed," she confessed. "But Lady Harker has not yet retired. She is in the drawing room if you are looking for her."

"I am not looking for my sister."

"No?" Sylvia wondered if he was in the habit of prowling the dark corridors of Pershing Hall at night. If so, she felt sorry for any hapless servants who might encounter him. Sebastian could really be quite intimidating when he chose.

Is that why he ventured out in the evening? To avoid interaction? Or was he merely restless after spending so much time confined to his apartments?

He did not look restless. In his rumpled black trousers and half-buttoned waistcoat, he looked exhausted. As if he were a man who had not slept for three days straight.

She searched his face. "You are not unwell, I hope?"

Sebastian stared down at her, his heavy scars appearing less severe in the soft glow from her candle. It occurred to her quite suddenly that she had yet to see him in full light. "Unwell," he repeated flatly.

His deep, emotionless voice sent a shiver of apprehension down her spine. She was on dangerous ground, she knew. "I meant...You are not in any pain, are you?"

He frowned. "I think not, Miss Stafford. Should I be?"

Sylvia looked up at him helplessly. What in heaven could she say? That Lady Harker had confided in her about his unhappy state upon returning from India? That she knew all about the pistol that he kept near his bedside? This was not the time or place, clearly, but if she was expected to do him any good during her brief stay at Pershing, at some point she would have to broach the subject of his injuries. One could not always speak in euphemisms and riddles, after all.

"No, of course not. I did not mean—" She broke off. "Forgive me. It is only that I have not seen you since the day of my arrival and I thought—"

His frown deepened. "You are my sister's guest, Miss Stafford, not mine."

"Yes, I know, but you might have at least joined us for dinner on occasion."

"To what purpose?"

She made a soft sound of exasperation. "Why, to eat, naturally. And to…to be around other people."

"Such as yourself."

She felt her color rising, but did not lower her gaze from his. "Such as myself."

"I see." He looked at her for a moment as if she were a frustrating puzzle that he could not solve. "My sister must be a poor hostess if you are pining for my company after only three days."

Sylvia stiffened at his choice of words. "Hardly pining, my lord."

Her displeasure only seemed to amuse him. A faintly ironic smile edged the scarred side of his mouth. "Tell me, Miss Stafford, how do you like Pershing Hall?"

"Very well, thank you," she replied, still very much on her dignity.

"I trust that my sister has made you comfortable here."

"Quite comfortable, my lord."

"And...everything is to your satisfaction?"

There was no mistaking the hesitation in his question. Sylvia's blue eyes briefly filled with confusion. Did it truly matter to him what she of all people thought of his ancestral home? Once she would have readily believed that it did. But she was no longer that same foolish girl. Sentiment had long since been replaced with hard common sense.

And common sense told her that Sebastian was merely seeking some sort of reassurance. Something to convince him that he could, indeed, find contentment at Pershing Hall. That there was no need to resort to drastic measures to alleviate his unhappiness.

"How could it not be?" she asked. "It is beautiful here, my lord. If it were my home, I would never wish to leave it."

Sebastian appeared rather startled for an instant. And then his expression hardened. "It is late, Miss Stafford," he said abruptly. "I have importuned you long enough."

"Oh, but you haven't—"

Before she could finish, he was gone, disappearing back into the darkness of the corridor without so much as a bow or a by your leave. Sylvia stared after him, utterly bewildered. What in the world could she possibly have said to offend him?

Chapter Six

Sebastian was not proud of himself for spying on Miss Stafford. It was a weakness. And he despised weakness, especially in himself. Even so, he could not resist the chance to look at her. Especially while remaining unseen himself. So, every morning on the way to his desk in his private sitting room, he stopped at the window overlooking the path where she had first ridden Ares so many days before. He leaned against the window frame, half-obscured by the heavy curtains, and he watched her.

Would that he could have left it at that.

Instead, he had been so monumentally stupid as to leave his apartments two nights before. It was then that he had seen Miss Stafford coming up the stairs. He had stepped back into the shadows, intending only to look at her, but she had stopped in the center of the hall, visibly upset. He had gone to her then, damned fool that he was, only to have his every suspicion about her confirmed.

"If it were my home," she had said, *"I would never wish to leave it."*

From anyone else, he would have taken it as a compliment of sorts, but from Miss Stafford it was something else entirely. It was, he believed, an invitation for him to *make* Pershing Hall her home. To make her the next Countess of Radcliffe.

Did she think he would so easily forget how cruelly she had discarded him when he was a mere second son? That he would simply succumb to her wiles? That he had no pride left at all?

And perhaps she was right, Sebastian thought grimly. For if he had any pride to speak of, he would not be gazing out the sitting room window now, waiting for Miss Stafford to appear on her morning ride.

It was stupid really. Nothing ever changed from day to day. She was always in the same blue riding habit, her figure set off to magnificent effect. She was always grave and quiet. As if she knew he watched her and was purposely denying him the pleasure of seeing her smile.

He dropped his gaze briefly to the lock of hair in his hand. The ribbon was faded and frayed along the edges, but the bound chestnut tresses still gleamed. He ran his thumb over them, almost meditatively, as he resumed his brooding vigil at the window.

Right on schedule, his sister's gray mare appeared in the distance. Beside her was Ares, the morning sun turning his bay coat to a shining copper.

But that was not all.

There was another horse with them this morning.

Sebastian stiffened. He had not been at Pershing Hall much over the last fifteen years, but one did not have to be a permanent resident of Hertfordshire to recognize Thomas Rotherham. He was the son of the Viscount Rotherham, the second largest landowner in the district. He was also reckoned a veritable Adonis around these parts. Tall, bronzed, and golden-haired. The village girls in Apsley Heath had been swooning over him for as long as Sebastian could remember.

How the devil had he known that Julia and Miss Stafford would be riding this morning?

Clenching his fist, Sebastian watched the three riders come into view. His eyes went straight to Miss Stafford. She was dressed exactly the same as every other morning, her beautiful face just as solemn and grave. But as he stared down at her, she turned her head to address Rotherham. The net veil on her little riding hat fluttered back from her wide blue eyes. And then she smiled.

Sebastian's heart stopped.

He had seen her smile at men like that three years ago in London. He had been jealous, of course, but he had known then that she was kind and civil to everyone, quick to laugh and always ready with a friendly word. It was why so many gentlemen had fallen in love with her. She had had a way about her that drew out the reticent fellows and put even the most nervous gentleman at his ease. She was, in short, pleasant company. "*A d-dashed good sort,*" he had heard one grateful young lord with a stammer declare after Miss Stafford partnered him in a dance.

He had never suspected that she had encouraged any of those men. He had never thought, not even for a moment, that she was a flirt.

He knew better now.

Later that morning, Sylvia strolled alone through the long picture gallery. Situated along the back of the house, it was lit by ten large windows that ran the length of the wall opposite. The midday sun filtered in, illuminating a collection of portraits that appeared to date as far back in time as the reign of the Tudors. Despite the hazy sunlight, it was a cold room—colder still in the shadowy expanses between the windows—and as she walked from one painting to the next, she tightened her old cashmere shawl more firmly about her shoulders.

There was no discernable order to the portraits. At least, not in terms of date. She observed a seventeenth century Van Dyck hanging next to an eighteenth century portrait of an angelic, fair-haired lady which looked to be the work of Thomas Gainsborough. Flanking that, was a relatively modern portrait of a handsome young gentleman who, upon closer inspection, could only be Sebastian's elder brother.

Like Sebastian, the man in the portrait was tall, lean, and broad-shouldered, with strongly hewn features and hair as black as a raven's wing. But there the similarity ended. Sebastian was stern and forbidding, while this painting showed a cheerful, devil-may-care sort of gentleman. A fellow who knew he was the heir to a title and a great fortune and had nothing at all to worry about in the world.

"My brother Edmund."

Sylvia gasped in alarm, spinning round to find Sebastian standing in the shadows at the opposite end of the gallery. "Lord Radcliffe!" She pressed a hand to her pounding heart. "You frightened me."

"The picture gallery is a frightening place, Miss Stafford. Did no one tell you? Generations of Conrad ghosts are said to walk here." He advanced upon her, stopping near enough for her to see the rigid set of his shoulders and the hard, unyielding line of his jaw. "Where is my sister?"

She took an instinctive step back from him. "Lady Harker is resting in her room."

"And you are wandering through my house alone."

"I am wandering through your picture gallery. I was not aware it was off limits."

He came closer still, finally stopping beside her to look up at the painting she had been studying. "My brother was but three and twenty when he sat for that portrait."

She turned her attention back to the painting, trying to ignore the growing sense of unease that made her pulse race. Sebastian was angry. Very angry. It fairly vibrated in the air around him. She affected not to notice. "You resemble each other," she said. "But I can see nothing of Lady Harker in either of you."

"Julia takes after my mother. There." He motioned to the portrait which she had thought to be a Gainsborough.

She stepped forward to examine it more closely. Sebastian's mother had a decidedly gentle air about her. Her mouth was curved into a beatific smile and, on her lap, she held a small, brown and white spaniel. "How beautiful she was," Sylvia murmured. Her eyes drifted over the lines and angles of the late Lady Radcliffe's face. "You're right. Lady Harker does favor her." She flicked a glance at him. "As do you, my lord."

Sebastian gave a derisive snort.

Sylvia frowned. "I'm quite serious." She gestured to the firm set of Lady Radcliffe's jaw. "There, you see."

"You have a fanciful imagination, Miss Stafford."

"I have no imagination," she said frankly. "I am sensible. It is my besetting sin."

"Are you sensible?" He turned to look at her, his lips pressed into a thin, furious line. "Judging by your behavior, I would say you are quite the opposite."

She looked up at him, startled. "I *beg* your pardon?"

"Do not misunderstand me. If you choose to play the flirt with every gentleman you meet in Cheapside, it is certainly no concern of mine. But when you are a guest in my home, madam, you are under my protection. And I'll not have it said that I stood idly by and allowed a lady—*a governess*—to be taken advantage of by my neighbor."

Sylvia's stomach dropped. For several seconds, she could do nothing but stare at him. There was so much in his speech to offend her that she scarcely knew where to begin. "Your neighbor?" she heard herself repeat faintly.

"Thomas Rotherham."

She clenched her fingers in the soft fabric of her shawl to stop their trembling. "What is it exactly that you are accusing me of?"

"I am not accusing you of anything, Miss Stafford. I am warning you. If you smile and bat your eyes at Rotherham, he will not respond with a proposal of marriage."

A scalding blush flooded her cheeks. "You are insulting, sir."

"I am doing you the courtesy of speaking plainly. Rotherham must know you are a governess. If you expect him to play the gentleman, you are very much mistaken."

"I have no expectations of Mr. Rotherham. Nor why should I have? I do not even know the man. We were introduced but briefly. I daresay we shall never meet again."

"He'll make a point of coming round now," Sebastian predicted darkly.

"I doubt that very much. And if he does, it will not be on my account. He is Lady Harker's friend, not mine. Indeed, I do not believe I exchanged more than five words with the man."

"It is not your words that concern me."

"What then?" she demanded. "What is this all about? I know I have done nothing improper."

"Do not try and deny it, Miss Stafford. I saw you with him this morning when you were riding along the edge of the park." He paused. "You were smiling at him."

If it were not so outrageous, she might have laughed. "Is that my great crime? Smiling at a gentleman?"

"Casting out lures, more like."

"Don't be absurd."

"You have no notion of the effect of your smiles," he said. "Or perhaps you do. Perhaps you employ them just as you do all of your other charms."

Sylvia was temporarily speechless. So this was his opinion of her. He thought her a flirt. A conniving sort of female set on entrapping innocent gentlemen into marriage. It was insulting and ridiculous, but—good lord!—is this what he thought she had done to him three years ago?

A shiver of realization turned her blood cold.

She took a steadying breath, exerting all of her effort to keep herself calm, to not succumb to the paralyzing embarrassment she felt at having to confront her past behavior. "I think you have a very poor opinion of me, my lord," she said, unable to hide the quaver in her voice. "Perhaps you have cause. But just because I was incautious once, it does not follow that I would behave in the same manner again. Indeed, I have never done so."

Sebastian's face darkened like a thundercloud. He took a step toward her. "Incautious," he repeated. "Is that what you call it?"

"No. I call it foolish. Childish. But I will not make excuses. It is in the past. I cannot undo it no matter how much I might wish to do so."

"I am not talking about the past. I am talking about today. About your behavior with Rotherham. The past has nothing at all to do with it."

"So you say, my lord. And yet, you have sketched the whole of my character from our acquaintance three years ago."

"When we met so briefly in London?" A bitter smile twisted the scarred side of his mouth into a sneer. "I am astonished you remember, Miss Stafford. It is so much ancient history to me."

She understood then that he meant to hurt her. That hurting her had been the goal of nearly every word uttered from the moment he entered the gallery. "I will not believe that you have forgotten," she said.

"Believe what you will, madam."

"At the very least, you must remember that we were friends once. That we—"

"The only thing that I remember about our former *acquaintance*," he interrupted coldly, "is that I had a fortunate escape."

His words cut straight to her heart, laying it open with the clinical skill of a Harley Street surgeon. She felt the humiliating sting of tears in her eyes. "Oh…" Her gaze fell from his. "Yes. I…I suppose that you did."

She turned away from him. Suddenly, she wanted nothing more than to be back in London, safe and secure in her attic bedroom at the Dinwiddy's modest house in Cheapside. At least there she knew which end was up. But running away would not solve anything. Especially not with so much unfinished between them. Besides, how was she to leave? Lady Harker would have to order the carriage. Either that or she would have to find a way to the railway station in Apsley Heath. Once there, she could purchase a ticket on the next train to London.

It was not impossible. Indeed, if she put her mind to the matter, she could probably leave as early as tomorrow morning.

In the meanwhile, she would have to settle for putting some distance between them.

"Miss Stafford," Sebastian said.

She imagined she heard a note of regret in his deep voice, but knew she was mistaken. It was only her treacherous heart hearing what it wanted to hear. Goodness knows it had led her astray with Sebastian before.

Ignoring him, she walked the short distance across the picture gallery to one of the tall, deeply set windows.

It was framed with heavy curtains pulled back to reveal an unobstructed view of the stark, north lawn. For all that it was cold outside, the sun was shining brightly. She stepped forward into its warm rays and looked out across the park.

He might have left the picture gallery then. Part of her hoped that he would. But he did not leave. He came to stand beside her, his large presence casting a dark shadow over the sunlit alcove.

She folded her arms across her midsection, feeling cold and utterly bereft beneath the staid propriety of her dark silk gown. Why would he not go? Why could he not leave her in peace? She hated him in that moment. Hated him for remaining at her side, for forcing his presence on her when she was at her most vulnerable.

At the same time, there was something unbearably intimate about the two of them there, so close in the window embrasure. It was an illusion, she knew, but it nevertheless compelled her to speak.

"I have often found myself wondering where it all went wrong between us," she said quietly. "Perhaps you were merely amusing yourself at my expense. Or perhaps...perhaps it was something I said in one of my letters."

"*What?*"

"I always suspected the latter," she admitted, "but I did not want to believe it. Now it seems that I owe you an apology, my lord. When I wrote to you as I did, I was under the impression that you and I…That we…That we had a mutual regard for each other." She swallowed, forcing herself to look up at him. He was staring down at her, white faced and still. His scars stood out in stark relief. "I am sorry if I shocked you or gave offense. And I do hope you have destroyed those letters. If not, I…I would ask that you give them back to me."

It was the most mortifying speech that Sylvia had ever made. She could only imagine how deeply she was blushing. She turned away from him to look out the window once more, fixing her gaze on a cluster of trees in the distance. After a time, she heard him clear his throat.

"What do you suppose there was in your letters that would have offended me?" he asked.

She gave a choked, humorless laugh. "Oh, where to begin?"

"Tell me."

"Let me see…Might it have been that I doused them with my perfume? Or perhaps it was that I closed each letter by sending you one thousand kisses?"

Sebastian said nothing for a long while.

A long while during which Sylvia fervently wished she had never come to Pershing Hall. She pressed her cheek to the window embrasure, closing her eyes in mortification.

"It was neither of those things," he said huskily.

"Oh. I see." She could say no more. For now she knew, beyond all doubt, what it was that had given him such a disgust of her. She supposed that she had always known. That dashed first letter! Was it any wonder he thought her a conscienceless flirt with an eye toward matrimony? She made herself look at him again. "I should never have written it."

Sebastian did not say anything. He merely looked down at her, as white faced and immobile as he had been before.

"It was three years ago," she said. "I was very green. Very stupid. And I daresay I thought…But that does not matter. It was a foolish thing to have written to you. And in my first letter, too. I hope we might agree to never think of it again. Indeed, I am deathly ashamed every time I do." She exhaled an unsteady breath. It was done. It was over. She had always wanted to know what it was that had ended their romance and now she did.

She could, at last, let him go.

"I believe I shall sit here awhile," she said, sinking down onto the window ledge. "If you would but give me a moment alone to collect my thoughts."

But he did not give her a moment alone. Instead, he sat down beside her, seemingly oblivious to the fact that he was subjecting himself to the full force of the midday sun. It shone a harsh light on his face, revealing every wretched scar.

"Do you still have them?" she asked. "My letters?"

"No."

She thought of the painstaking hours she had spent writing them. Of all the hope and affection she had poured into every line. "Yes well..." She felt suddenly as if she might cry. "I daresay there was nothing in them worth saving."

Sebastian made no reply.

Sylvia was beginning to feel that she was having a conversation with herself. Why had he sat down beside her if he did not mean to talk? Was he simply going to stare at her until she burst into tears?

But perhaps he had already said too much? Perhaps it hurt him to speak? The scar from the saber cut that had damaged half his face travelled down to the top of his black cravat. She had never properly seen its full horror until now, had never truly comprehended just how severe it really was. Had it damaged his throat as well? Was that why he always sounded so raspy and hoarse?

"Why could you not have been more careful?" she asked.

Sebastian's color heightened almost imperceptibly.

"It was one of the last things I said to you, do you remember? *Promise me that you will be careful,*" she echoed her long ago words. "Of course you don't remember. It is all nothing more than ancient history to you.

Unimportant and long forgotten. But I wish...Oh, I wish you had not been hurt."

"As does everyone who must look upon me now," he said. "My face is not a pleasant sight."

"That is not what I meant. I meant...I wish you had not been *hurt*. No matter what has passed between us...I cannot bear to think of you in pain."

Sebastian fell silent again, but she could see a muscle working in his jaw. The subject of his injuries was upsetting to him. Perhaps she should not have mentioned it. Perhaps she should have simply pretended that he looked the same as he always had. That nothing had changed.

"And as for your injuries being unpleasant," she said before she could stop herself. "When I first saw you this way ...When I was standing in the hall outside your rooms...To own the truth, I was more alarmed by your state of undress than anything else." She turned to look out the window, feeling the weight of his stare on her face as she did so. "Have you really kept that lock of hair I gave you?"

He did not answer.

She watched a servant walking across the lawn far down below. The gardener, she thought absently. Pershing Hall was a large estate. No doubt there were hundreds of servants.

"Your sister misunderstood everything. She thought you had kept it because you cared for me. I tried to explain to her that many soldiers keep a token of that sort, but she would not credit it. '*If your hair has given him comfort,*' she said, '*only think how much it will help him if you are there in person.*'" She cast another fleeting glance at Sebastian. "She cares for you very much."

"She is an infernal nuisance."

Silvia's mouth lifted in a sudden half smile. "She was going to hire a private enquiry agent to find me."

"Good God."

"Luckily, there are many who still remember my unhappy fate after the scandal. Lady Harker was able to locate me, at last. In Cheapside. The horror!"

"Where you are a governess to two little girls."

"Clara and Cora. The dearest children you would ever care to meet." Her smile broadened, revealing the rare sight of her two dimples. Sebastian's gaze dropped briefly down to her mouth, an arrested look on his face. "I have taught them to perform for company," she said. "Clara, the eldest, plays a ballad on the piano and Cora, her little sister, sings. It is more endearing than accomplished, I admit. But they have learned so much and make me very proud of them."

"You were ever fond of children," he observed gruffly.

Her smile slowly faded. She had once thought to have children of her own. With him. "A trait that has served me well in my new life," she said.

"Your father left no provision for you at all?"

"No. Nothing. I found out afterward that he was deeply in debt. He had borrowed from friends and even the moneylenders. He wagered everything in that last game. I daresay he would have wagered me, too, if he had thought of it in time."

"And your relations?"

"I wrote to them…afterward. Only one of them replied. Papa's sister, a woman whom I have never met. She has twelve children, if you can credit it. Seven of them still in the nursery. She invited me to come and stay at her home in Northumberland. I believe she hoped to make an unpaid servant of me. A drudge. I decided then and there that if I must be in service, I may as well earn a wage."

"So now you teach a merchant's children to play and sing. In Cheapside." Sebastian's fist clenched where it lay on his thigh. "Do you never sing yourself anymore?"

"I sometimes sing lullabies to Clara and Cora when they cannot sleep."

"That is not what I meant."

"I know what you meant." Sylvia turned her gaze back to the window. "The answer is no, my lord. I do not sing anymore. Not in the way that I did before Papa died. There are no musical evenings at Mr. and Mrs. Dinwiddy's house and no Penelope Mainwaring to accompany me on the piano. Excepting lullabies, I do not sing at all. Not even for myself."

"There is a music room here."

"Oh?"

"If Julia accompanies you, perhaps you might sing as you once did."

She looked at him again, achingly aware that his own gaze had never wavered. It was then that she saw that the haughty, sneering expression with which he had regarded her for much of their conversation was strangely absent. She wondered when it had gone—and when it would come back again. "Tonight?"

"Any night."

A troubled frown knit her brow. "Does that mean I am welcome to remain here at Pershing Hall? After everything you said to me, I assumed—"

"I lost my temper," he said. "I will not pretend it was the first time."

It was not an apology, though Sylvia suspected it was as close to one as she was likely to receive from him. Even so, it was not enough. "You hurt me with what you said."

He failed to conceal a wince. "Miss Stafford, I—"

"Did you think that I could not be hurt?" she asked. "Did you think that because I am a servant now that I would not feel it here" —she pressed her hand to her heart— "every time you speak to me as if you hate me?"

Sebastian's expression darkened with something very like anguish. For several seconds, her words hung heavy in the silence between them.

"I don't hate you," he said finally. "I have never hated you."

Sylvia's lower lip wobbled. She turned away from him, blinking back the fresh sting of tears. "H-Haven't you?"

"No," he said. And then more strongly, "*No*." He leaned closer to her, crushing her heavy skirts beneath his leg. She felt his warm breath brush against her hair. "I spoke cruelly, Miss Stafford. It was badly done of me."

"I did not deserve it."

"No. You did not. I should never have addressed you as I did. And if you will forgive me…"

A faint spark of hope kindled in Sylvia's breast. "Are you apologizing to me, sir?"

"I am," he said. His voice roughened. "I don't want you to leave."

His words brought a flush of color to her cheeks. She closed her eyes for a moment. And then she turned to face him. "I thought it was a mistake to come here," she confessed. "But if there was a way to put the unfortunate past behind us…A way to start again. As friends. We *were* friends once, were we not? Before that stupid letter?"

He gave her another long, searching look. "We *were* friends, Miss Stafford," he said. "And I very much hope we will be so again."

Chapter Seven

Julia found them in the picture gallery only a short time later. She was in extraordinarily high spirits, which she claimed were a result of having had an "excellent rest," but which Sebastian knew were really a consequence of having discovered him alone with Miss Stafford. His sister was never so cheerful as when she thought one of her interfering schemes was successfully coming to fruition.

She tried to persuade him to join them downstairs for tea. He scarcely heard her. His mind was in turmoil. He made his excuses and, with a level of civility that plainly astonished his sister, he took his leave of them. Minutes later, he was safely ensconced in his private sitting room, seated in front of the hearth with a very large glass of brandy in his hand. He stared unseeing into the fire.

Miss Stafford had sent him letters.

Perfumed letters sealed with a thousand kisses.

Could it be true? A clever woman might make up such a tale to convince him that she had cared for him all along. A convenient story now that he was the Earl of Radcliffe.

But Miss Stafford had not been lying. He had seen that plainly enough. She had been deeply mortified. Confound it, she had been *hurt*. But she had not been dishonest. She had, apparently, never been dishonest.

The realization was staggering.

It still did not explain the rest of it, however. The mysterious something that she had written in her first letter—the something for which she believed that *he* had ended their romance. What the devil? He could not even begin to fathom what that something might have been.

He had received no letters from Sylvia Stafford. Not a single, solitary one.

It had taken a year for him to accept that no letter was ever going to come. That she had never intended to write to him. That everything between them had, very likely, existed solely in his own fevered, romantic brain. Even then he had still held fast to her blasted lock of hair, the one emblem of warmth and hope in that wretched hellhole.

But there *had* been letters.

And she had come here believing that *he* was the one who had abandoned *her*. "*She said that I was mistaken,*" Julia had told him. "*That you did not care for her.*"

Bloody hell.

He took a large swallow of brandy, remembering the look on her face when she had turned to him and asked for her letters back. She had seemed to have no notion of the devastating effect of her words. Her attention had been fully consumed with apologizing for having ever written in the first place.

Apologizing. To *him*.

Sebastian did not know whether to laugh or to weep. He settled instead for muttering a long, and particularly eloquent, oath.

Milsom whistled appreciatively as he entered the sitting room. "What's roused your temper, sir?"

"Nothing." Sebastian finished his glass of brandy and began to pour another.

"Nothing, my lord?" Milsom gave a huff of disbelief. "Don't think I've heard you use language like that since that drunken doctor was stitching up your face outside of Jhansi."

Sebastian leaned his head against the back of his chair with a low groan. "Not now, Milsom."

Milsom was not deterred. "You stormed out of here in a right temper," he said. "The second footman says you were looking for Miss Stafford."

"The second footman can go straight to the devil—and you along with him. This has nothing to do with either of you."

"Ah," Milsom said knowingly. "A lovers' quarrel, was it?"

Sebastian did not deny it. He took another drink. "If you must know," he said, "she claims to have sent me letters."

Milsom stopped where he stood. "So, she wrote to you after all, did she?"

Sebastian stared meditatively down at his half-filled glass. "It would seem so."

Milsom's foxlike face broke into a broad grin. "And didn't I tell you she must have done? What with the post gone astray and us marching up and down the—"

"The post did not go astray."

"Beg pardon, my lord? Then why—" Milsom's words were interrupted by a light rap sounding on the door.

This time when Sebastian cursed, he did not mutter. "That will be my sister."

Sure enough, when Milsom answered the door, it was Julia who popped her head in. "May I come in for a moment?" she asked.

Sebastian doubted whether anything could stop her. He motioned to the chair opposite his with a peremptory wave of his hand.

Her face brightened considerably. She hurried into the room to join him, settling herself on the edge of the chair he had indicated. "Well?" she demanded.

Milsom quietly withdrew back into the bedroom, closing the doors behind him.

Sebastian pressed his handkerchief to the scarred side of his mouth as he raised his glass for another drink. "I thought you were having tea."

"That was over an hour ago!" She cast a disapproving glance at the half-empty bottle of brandy on the table beside him. "It is no wonder you have lost track of the time. You should not drink so much. Papa never did."

"Our father drank exactly enough to get him through the day." He took another swallow of brandy. "As do I."

"Well, I daresay Papa's days were not as trying as yours."

"No doubt."

"But I cannot like it, Sebastian. Especially when you are making so much progress with Miss Stafford. You must not ruin your chances with her by becoming intoxicated."

Two glasses of brandy was a fair way from being intoxicated, but Sebastian did not argue the point. "Where is Miss Stafford?"

"She is waiting for me downstairs in the drawing room. I am supposed to be fetching my paints and canvas. We are going to walk down to the bridge. Will you come with us?"

"No."

"Not even to see Miss Stafford? I promise I will not chaperone you too closely. Indeed, you will scarcely know I am there."

Sebastian frowned into the fire. The truth was he would have liked nothing better than to see Miss Stafford again. Unfortunately, if he were to go out of doors on such a sunny day as this, *she* would also have to see *him*. It was bad enough that he had already exposed himself in the light of the picture gallery window. God only knew what Miss Stafford was thinking of him now that she had got a proper look at his face. "Another time, perhaps," he said vaguely.

He waited for his sister to leave, but she remained where she was, regarding him with the same bright, hopeful expression. "Did you really sit with her in the picture gallery, Sebastian?"

"As you observed."

"And you were civil to her the whole time?"

His chest rose and fell on a ragged breath. Damn it all, he had not been civil to her. He had been a brute. A beast. He had thought he had cause, but now, after what Miss Stafford had told him, he was no longer sure of anything. He drained his glass and set it down on the table beside him. "What was Thomas Rotherham doing with you this morning?" he asked abruptly.

Julia's smile dimmed. "Doing with us? Why… nothing. He only accompanied us on our ride."

"And how did he know that you were going riding?"

For the barest instant his sister appeared to be on the verge of an elaborate falsehood. Then her shoulders slumped. "I sent a note round to Moreton Grange," she confessed. "I invited him to come with us."

Sebastian ran a hand over his face. His head was beginning to pound. "Dare I ask why?"

"I thought…if you saw him with her…" She gave him a rueful look. "I hoped you might be jealous."

The fire crackled ominously in the grate.

"And it worked, did it not? You and Miss Stafford have reunited and—" Julia broke off uncertainly. "You have, haven't you? Miss Stafford has not confided in me, but surely you must have reconciled with her, else you would not have been sitting so close together in the picture gallery. And without a chaperone, too!"

Sebastian fixed his sister with an implacable glare. "I have half a mind to write to Harker and tell him what you've been up to."

She shrugged. "I would not care if you did. Harker does not mind my matchmaking. Especially when I have done it to help my very own brother."

"Does he not?" Sebastian's deep voice lowered to a menacing rumble. "If you were *my* wife I would thrash you within an inch of your life."

Julia's mouth fell open, her expression transforming into one of almost comical dismay. "You would never thrash your own wife!"

"And lock her in her room, too," he added for good measure.

"I do not believe you," she said. "You would never hurt a woman."

Sebastian recalled the devastated look in Miss Stafford's eyes when he had told her that he had had a fortunate escape three years ago. "You think not?"

"No," Julia said. "And I don't see why you should be so cross with me! Everything I have done has been for your benefit. Why, only last week, Miss Stafford was ready to return to Cheapside. She would have done so, too, if I had not tricked you out of your rooms today."

"She's decided to stay, I take it."

"She has not said so," Julia admitted. "But I hope she has. Perhaps if you were to tell her that *you* wished her to stay?"

He dug his fingers into the folds of his cravat and began to tug it loose. "I have already told her so."

"You have?" Julia clasped her hands to her bosom. "Oh, Sebastian! I knew you would wish to see her. And I knew that I must convince her to come here, whatever I must say to do so. Even if I must tell the tiniest little lie or two."

Sebastian stilled, suddenly alert. "What lies?"

"Oh...you know."

He dropped his hand from his cravat. "No, I do not know," he said. "Pray enlighten me."

Julia affected to be wholly occupied with smoothing out an invisible wrinkle in the skirts of her blossom pink muslin gown. "It was nothing of note. Only the veriest commonplace."

"What lies, Julia?" he asked again.

"Well..." She hesitated. "I told her that I was in an interesting condition."

He scowled. "Why in blazes would you tell her that?"

"Because if I were indeed expecting, then Harker would fuss over me like an old mother hen." She raised her eyes to his face, offering a sheepish smile. "I said that he worried about my being upset by the situation here at Pershing. Because of how it would affect the baby."

"The situation," Sebastian repeated.

"She understood at once, of course. And that was when she agreed to accompany me back to Hertfordshire."

"What situation?"

Julia shook her head. "I do not wish to say. You will not like it."

"What did you tell her?" he thundered.

"You needn't shout at me, Sebastian! I know I should not have done it. But she would not have come otherwise. So you must see why—"

"I shall count to five and if you have not answered me, then I am going to pitch you out of that window."

Julia leapt up, scurrying strategically behind her chair as Sebastian began to count. "I told her that I feared you would do something stupid!" she blurted out.

He was on his feet in an instant, looming over her. "*What*?"

"I said that you kept a pistol beside your bed this whole last year and that—" Julia gave a loud yelp as her brother lunged at her. She sprinted out of his reach, darting toward the door. "I had to!" she cried. "And I am not sorry!" And then she bolted from the sitting room as fast as her legs would carry her.

Chapter Eight

It was well past one in the morning. Sylvia did not need a clock to tell her so. She had been tossing and turning for hours, too restless to fall back asleep. Earlier, after a brief episode of tears, she had dozed fitfully, only to wake feeling as forlorn and miserable as she had when she first retired to her bedroom for the evening. It had seemed stupid to cry. Everything was sorted out now, was it not? Sebastian had said that he did not hate her. That he had never hated her. He had even said that he hoped they might be friends again.

Yet, he had not joined them on their walk. Nor had he joined them for dinner. And as for coming to the music room to listen to her sing…

She had been a fool to have believed that he would. If she had been thinking with her head instead of her heart, she would have recognized at once that his kind words in the picture gallery were nothing more than empty civility. He clearly did not want to see her any more than was necessary. No doubt she had made him uncomfortable with all her talk of those letters.

Sylvia rolled onto her back and stared at the canopy over her bed. She contemplated returning to Cheapside in the morning. It would not be running away, surely. And no one could ever accuse her of cowardice. She had, after all, managed an entire week at Pershing Hall. One wonderful, terrible week in which she had been confronted by all the memories of her former life. But there was a limit to what one could endure and, unless she was very much mistaken, she had reached that limit last night. She feared that if she stayed any longer, she would become truly, and irrevocably, unhappy.

She tossed and turned for another quarter of an hour. Then, abruptly, she flung off her blankets and sat up. She was done with lying awake and worrying. If she could not sleep, she may as well go down and find something to read. She rose from bed and put on her dressing gown, cinching it tightly round her waist. Her hair had worked itself loose from its nighttime plait and now fell loose about her shoulders. She did not regard it. No one else would be up. The house had been deathly quiet for hours.

Lighting a candle, she quietly exited her bedchamber and made her way downstairs.

The Pershing Hall library was a singularly masculine room, dark and cluttered and smelling faintly of pipe tobacco and lemon oil and beeswax furniture polish. She had not been back to it since the day of her arrival. Lady Harker preferred to serve refreshments in the much brighter, and far more feminine, drawing room. Nevertheless, during the short time she had spent having tea with Sebastian and Lady Harker that first afternoon, she had not failed to notice that the library contained a dazzling array of books. She was certain to find something interesting to read.

She placed her candle on an inlaid table near one of the bookcases. It cast a small halo of light, barely enough for her to see the titles engraved on the spines of the books. She peered up from shelf to shelf, skimming scholarly and political tomes, volumes on classical Greece, and the odd book on agriculture. She was beginning to think she would have to content herself with the story of Hector and Achilles or some such thing when, on the top shelf, far out of reach, she spied a beautifully bound copy of one of Mr. Dickens' novels.

It was *David Copperfield*. Sylvia remembered having read the novel years ago when it was first released in serial form. It had been excessively diverting. She cast about the room for a library ladder and found one leaning alongside the shelves several rows over. Having retrieved it, she set it carefully against the shelves in front of her, tested the first rung with one slippered foot, and began to climb.

The rickety ladder creaked beneath her, but she paid it no mind. She did not weigh very much and she would only be standing on the rungs for the briefest moment. She continued up, bracing one hand on a bookshelf as she went.

The ceilings at Pershing Hall were ungodly high. She had not realized just how high until she had begun to climb. She reached out with her free hand, stretching her arm full length toward the desired book. It was still not quite within her grasp. More determined than ever, she climbed up the final step to the very top of the ladder. She reached out again toward the book, straining to touch the edge of its spine with her fingertips.

The ladder wobbled precariously.

Sylvia gasped in alarm. She nimbly set one foot on a lower bookshelf to steady herself. It was not one second too soon. The library ladder gave way beneath her, clattering to the floor.

She was left clinging to the bookshelves like a monkey.

Her heart raced, her palms suddenly sweaty as they gripped the shelf. She took a deep breath to calm herself. Whatever else her failings, she was not impractical. She could see immediately that there was nothing for it. She would have to climb down, feeling her way from shelf to shelf.

She chanced a glance downward. The library floor seemed a very long way away. She was not unduly afraid of heights, but she had a great respect for the frailty of the human body. Only four years ago she had sprained her ankle jumping down from a stile. It had taken weeks to heal. If she were to hurt herself here, at Pershing Hall, there would be no more chance of leaving early.

She peered down again, spying the shelf immediately below the one that she was standing on. It was not so far. She would simply proceed slowly and carefully….

A sudden draft caused her candle to flicker.

"Don't you dare go out," she warned it. It was going to be difficult enough as it was to climb down these dratted shelves. To do so in the pitch dark would be almost impossible.

Just then a light shone into the room. She turned her head, hoping against hope that it was a footman or one of the housemaids. "Is someone there?" she called out.

"Miss Stafford?" Sebastian's deep voice echoed from the library door.

At the sound of it, Sylvia closed her eyes in horror. "Oh God," she groaned. "It needed only that."

Sebastian was accustomed to making swift decisions in times of crisis, but at the sight of Sylvia Stafford perched precariously on the library bookshelves, he experienced a split second of absolute dismay. She was wearing nothing but a thin dressing gown over an equally thin nightgown, the hems of which were both lifted to expose her shapely bare ankles and dainty, slippered feet. As if that were not enough to knock his world off its axis, her dark, chestnut hair was unbound. It fell all about her in magnificent disarray, reaching almost to her waist. Her incredibly slender, uncorseted waist. Good God, he could probably span it with two hands.

And it looked like he just might have to.

"Don't move," he commanded, striding toward her.

Miss Stafford glanced down at him. She was blushing mightily. "I was attempting to reach a book on the top shelf when the ladder collapsed."

"Never mind it," he said gruffly. He set the branch of candles he was carrying on a nearby table and, without breaking stride, swept up a heavy wooden chair in his hand. He placed it firmly on the carpeted floor below her. It easily bore his weight as he sprang onto the seat and reached up to catch her round the waist. He felt her inhale a tremulous breath as his fingers pressed into her flesh. She was very high up. Tall as he was, he could scarcely get a secure grip on her. "If you will put a hand on my shoulder, I will swing you down."

She slowly released her grip on the bookshelf, stretching one hand down toward his shoulder. "I cannot reach you."

"It's all right, just…let me—"

Before he could finish his sentence, Miss Stafford's foot slipped on the lower shelf. She fell with a startled cry. He caught her directly. She was in no real danger. Even so, she flung her arms around his neck, clinging to him for dear life.

"I have you," he said. He stepped down from the chair and slowly lowered her to the ground, painfully aware of every inch of her body sliding down the front of his until her feet touched safely on the library floor.

He might have released her then, but her limbs were a trifle unsteady. At least, that is what he told himself. It may or may not have been the case. In any event, he did not have the will to let her go.

And, for whatever reason, she did not let him go either.

Instead, she looked up at him, a little dazed. "How *mortifying*," she whispered.

It had been years since Sebastian had laughed. There had, in truth, been very little to laugh about. But at Miss Stafford's words, he felt his lips quiver with reluctant amusement. "Indeed," he said.

Her own mouth quivered in return. For a moment she valiantly attempted to suppress her mirth. And then, overcome, she bent her head against his chest and gave way to an outpouring of laughter.

It was a low, merry sound that warmed him all the way to his soul. Unthinking, he removed his hands from her waist and put his arms around her, drawing her into an embrace. He rested his face lightly against her hair. It felt like heaven against his cheek, as silky and thick as the lock he always carried with him.

"What a spectacle I'm making of myself," she gasped between laughs. "I fear I am hysterical."

Sebastian's heart was thundering, his blood pulsing hot in his veins. His body, at least, had not forgotten how to respond to her nearness. His mind, on the other hand, was all chaos and confusion. He had questions. Concerns. Not the least of which was that he was presently taking advantage of an unmarried female guest under his own roof.

"Nonsense," he said. "It was a humorous predicament."

She drew back from him, sliding her arms from around his neck to rest her hands lightly on his chest. "You're not laughing."

"I'm laughing on the inside," he said. At that, she gave him a dimpled smile. But he did not smile in return. He could not. His heart ached too much. And he was suddenly, horribly conscious of how monstrous he must look to her now that their faces were only inches apart.

Miss Stafford's own smile faded slowly. She moved to extricate herself from his grasp and he immediately let her go. She stepped away from him, directing her attention to straightening her rumpled dressing gown. "I should not have ventured from my room."

"Why not? You are a guest here, not a prisoner."

"I'll wager none of your other guests ever found themselves in the ridiculous predicament I was just in."

"No," Sebastian admitted. "Not that I am aware." He watched as she re-tied the fabric belt of her dressing gown, her slim hands knotting it snugly at her waist.

"I did not think so," Miss Stafford said. She smoothed her hand once more over the skirts of her dressing gown before wandering toward the old Vaugondy library globe that stood in a recess between two of the bookcases. "I suppose that this incident will tally nicely with that foolish letter I wrote you."

He went still, taken off guard by her words.

"Indeed," she said as she touched her finger to the globe and gave it a slow, deliberate half-spin in its stout wooden frame. "I seem to have a rare talent for making an idiot of myself where you are concerned."

Sebastian clenched one hand at his side. Is that what she believed? That he held her in contempt? That he thought her a fool?

More than ever he wished that he knew what was in that blasted first letter. In the picture gallery, he had been sorely tempted to tell her that he had never received it. That he had never received any of her letters. But something had stopped him. It was not disbelief. He was almost certain now that she *had* written to him. However, if she had known—if she had even suspected—that he had never received a single solitary letter, would she have confessed to him as much as she already had about the contents of those long lost missives?

He doubted it.

And then he would never have known. The knowledge was painful, true. Indeed, reflecting on the year of heartsick torment he had spent in India, wondering why she had never written, wondering what he had said or done to lose her affections—or worse, whether he had ever had her affections in the first place—was what had kept him up most of the night. If only he had realized then that somewhere out there were letters written to him by Sylvia Stafford! Perfumed letters sealed with a thousand kisses! But where? What in blazes had happened to them?

He raked a hand through his already disheveled black hair. "So much for putting the unfortunate past behind us."

"I'm sorry," she said quietly. "I should not have mentioned it, but I. . . ." Her voice quavered. "I cannot forget."

"Nor can I," he said.

She looked up from the globe and met his eyes. "Then I suppose there is nothing left to be said, is there?"

Sebastian's expression hardened with resolve. There *was* something more to be said, by God, and he knew that he must be the one to say it. He took a decisive step toward her and stopped. His heart was thudding heavily in his chest. He had the sense that he was standing on the edge of a great precipice. What was at the bottom, he could not see. It would be a leap of faith. There was no choice but to take it. "Miss Stafford," he said, "I never received any of your letters."

Chapter Nine

Sylvia's hand fell from the globe. She turned sharply to look at him. "*I beg your pardon?*"

Sebastian's face was grim. "The letters you wrote to me. I never received a single one. Indeed, until this morning, when you mentioned your letters in the picture gallery, I believed that you had not written at all. It is why I was…uncivil…to you when you first arrived at Pershing."

She stared at him in disbelief. "That cannot be true," she said. "You knew about my letters. We discussed them."

"*You* discussed them. I merely encouraged you. Selfish of me, I know. I should have told you the truth the moment I understood it for myself, but I—" He broke off with a low sound of frustration. "I wanted to know what you had written. I did not think you would admit to anything if you realized your letters had never come."

She frantically thought back to the conversation they had had as they sat together in the window embrasure. What in heaven had she told him?

"None of them came?" she asked faintly. "Not a single one?"

"None," he said. "And all of my own letters were returned unopened."

"*Your* letters?" Sylvia's knees weakened.

Sebastian was instantly at her side. His strong arm encircled her waist, enfolding her in the scent of spiced bergamot, starched linen, and clean male skin. "Come," he said. "We had better sit."

She allowed him to steer her to the large, velvet-cushioned settee near the fireplace. He kept his hand at her back as she sat down, watching with uncommon alertness as she drew the folds of her dressing gown more firmly around her. It was unconsciously done. Modesty was the last thing on her mind. When Sebastian sank down beside her, she hardly registered the impropriety of how close they were to each other. "What do you mean, *your* letters?" she asked.

"The letters I wrote to you from India," he said. "They were returned to me unopened. Every last one of them."

Her heart twisted. "You wrote to me," she whispered.

"Frequently." His somber expression briefly reflected a glimmer of the anguish in her own. "And you wrote to me, apparently."

"Often."

"And sealed your letters with a thousand kisses."

Oh God! She looked away from him. "D-did I tell you that?" Her eyes closed briefly against a flood of embarrassment. "I'm sorry. My head is spinning."

"It is a lot to take in."

"Yes. I still cannot..." She tried to put her feelings into words, but it was all a jumble. "When you never answered, I thought...I thought..."

"I know what you thought," he said. "It was what I thought as well. I expect it is what he wanted us to think."

"That we hated each other."

"Worse. That we had forgotten each other."

She pressed a hand to her face, struggling desperately to make sense of it all. "Wait..." Her disordered thoughts caught on one phrase and held. "Who are you talking about? Who is *he*?"

"Your father, obviously."

Sylvia's breath stopped. "No," she said. It was not true. It couldn't be. If Sebastian had known her father better, he would never have suggested such a thing. "Papa would not have interfered."

"You think not?"

"He had no reason," she said. "It was he who gave me permission to write to you."

For the barest instant, Sebastian could not hide his astonishment. And then his expression shuttered. "Did he, indeed," he said. There was an underlying current of anger in his voice.

"Yes." Her words tumbled out more quickly as she rose to Papa's defense. "He saw how distressed I was when you returned to India. He told me not to worry. That you would return in no time at all. He even gave me his morning papers each day at breakfast so that I could search for news of you to put my mind at ease."

Sebastian stilled. "You looked for news of me in the papers?"

A self-conscious blush rose in her cheeks. "Of course, I did. I checked for your name every day. I was terrified that you would be hurt or killed. And then, when I heard nothing from you, I thought you must have been. It did not even occur to me until much later that you simply had no wish to write to me." She exhaled slowly. "Or so I believed."

He looked at her for a long time, a bewildering series of emotions crossing his face. "I still cannot believe that your father permitted *you* to write to *me*."

"Why not? He knew that we were friends. And he was not unsympathetic to a soldier's need for letters from home." She paused, adding, "Surely you must realize by now that Papa was not a high stickler."

"In my experience," Sebastian said dryly, "even the most ramshackle fellow can transform into a high stickler when it comes to his own daughter."

Sylvia's brows knit in an apprehensive frown. She looked down at her lap, trying to think of a way to explain to Sebastian that Papa could have had nothing to do with any of it. It must have been an error with the post, she thought, or something to do with the unreliability of mail delivery in India. But the more she puzzled over it, the less certain she became.

Her father made a rather obvious villain. He was in debt. Serious enough debt that he would take his own life a year later. He had a strong motive for her to marry well. Specifically, to marry one of her wealthier admirers—Lord Goddard, perhaps. If he had thought she was in danger of marrying a comparatively poor soldier, he could easily have taken steps to prevent her from forming what he believed to be an undesirable attachment.

But if he had objected to her burgeoning romance with Sebastian, why on earth had Papa given her permission to correspond with him? Unless…

Unless he had known that to forbid her outright was the surest way to guarantee that she would take the bit between her teeth and do exactly as she pleased.

No. It would have been a much better strategy to make her believe that her gentleman of choice had cruelly abandoned her. That he had, perhaps, merely been amusing himself at her expense during the London season.

She shook her head, refusing to believe it. Papa had been selfish. Reckless. But a deception such as this passed all bounds. "He wouldn't have done such a thing," she insisted, as much to herself as to Sebastian. "Not to me."

Sebastian looked wholly unconvinced. "Did he ever give you any indication that he objected to my suit?"

Sylvia lifted one shoulder in a helpless shrug. "He did question me, naturally, but he was not unreasonable and, in the end, he said that he trusted me and I may do as I liked."

"How very obliging of him," he said. "Did it never occur to you that he might have read your letters?"

"No. Why should it? He had no opportunity to do so."

Sebastian's gaze narrowed. "Not even when he posted them?"

Sylvia had the oddest sensation that his question was not what it seemed. She answered it anyway, telling him the truth—for better or for worse. "My father did not post my letters," she said. "*I* did."

Sebastian drew back in blank dismay. "*You*?"

Miss Stafford gave him a puzzled look. "Yes." She paused. "Well, at least, my maid did."

Her maid. He felt a palpable wave of relief. Without conscious thought, he rubbed the scarred side of his face.

She watched him with swift concern. "Does it hurt very much?"

He immediately dropped his hand. They were sitting perilously close. Close enough that she could see his scars, even in the candlelight. He felt a rush of intense embarrassment. "Not significantly."

"Lady Harker said that you have been prescribed laudanum, but that you refuse to take it."

"Did she? I am not surprised. My sister has informed me that she told you a great many things in order to lure you here. Most of which are patently untrue."

"Oh?"

"For one, it may interest you to know that my sister is not in an interesting condition, as she puts it. For another, I do not keep a pistol at my bedside. Nor do I entertain thoughts of blowing my brains out."

For an instant, Miss Stafford looked stunned. "My goodness," she said. And then, very slowly, her mouth curved into a smile. A genuine smile, dimples and all. "And to think I thought her a bit silly to begin with."

"Only a bit?"

"Yet she knew precisely what to say to get me to come here. Worried that you might do something stupid, indeed. And to say that she had found you weeping while clutching a lock of my hair! How gullible I am."

Sebastian turned a dull red. Curse and confound his sister! Had she really told Sylvia Stafford *that*? Not that it wasn't true. He *had* been weeping and holding a lock of her hair. But the tears had come after waking from a particularly terrible nightmare about the uprising. And he had been holding her lock of hair in his hand because it always calmed him during times of great stress.

"Julia should not have lied to you," he said. "Not about something like that."

"I think your sister would say or do anything to help you. You are quite lucky in that regard."

"Lucky, am I?" One corner of his mouth hitched up as he recollected Julia sprinting from his rooms earlier that afternoon. "When she told me what she had done, I nearly throttled her."

"I am glad she told you," Miss Stafford said. "And I am glad things are not as dire as she described them."

"Is that the only reason you agreed to come? To prevent me from putting a period to my existence?"

"In large part, yes. Though I am not sure what I could have done to prevent it. Especially when you have spent most of my visit avoiding me." Her fingertips traced absently along the lines of the embroidered seat cushion at her side. "Why did you not join us for dinner this evening?"

Sebastian's shattered senses sounded a dull warning. He dismissed it as a false alarm. "Because I had a paper to finish for the philosophical society." It was not entirely a lie. He had spent most of the evening toiling over that blasted paper. "Why? What sinister motive did you assign to me?"

"I thought you did not wish to be in company with me."

"A foolish assumption."

"Is it? After how you've sneered at me since the day I arrived?"

Sebastian winced. "Have I sneered?"

"You know that you have."

"Then I must beg your pardon." What else could he say? That he had sought to punish her for rejecting him? That he had wished to humble her? To show her how little she had meant to him then and how much less she meant to him now?

In the process, he had been more than insulting. He had been purposefully cruel. It had been childish of him and damnably uncivil.

He was heartily ashamed of himself.

"Miss Stafford…I know you have ample reason to think otherwise," he said, "but I don't want you to leave Pershing Hall. Not yet. I meant what I said when I told you that I hoped we might be friends again."

She considered this for a moment. "I suppose, then, that if I stay the rest of the month—"

"*If* you stay?" He was at once both incredulous and outraged. "What do you mean *if*?"

"There is no point in remaining the rest of the month if you continue to avoid me. If I stay, you must join us downstairs on occasion."

"Haven't I been doing so?"

"Darkened libraries and shadowy portrait galleries are not enough, I'm afraid."

Sebastian did not need her to spell it out for him. She wanted the daylight. She wanted to see him, laid bare, in all his beastly glory. The prospect sunk his spirits. Is this what it would take to keep her here? To once again win her heart? His voice deepened with bitterness at the unfairness of it all. "The very thing you ask of me is the thing that will drive you away."

Miss Stafford's eyes softened with compassion. "You do me an injustice."

"Do I? When I returned from India, my own sister screamed and fainted."

"I am not your sister, my lord."

"Of that, madam, I am well aware."

Her color heightened. "Yes, well...It seems to me that you worry about your appearance a great deal too much."

Sebastian stiffened. It was the truth, of course. He had never been a vain man, but he despised the sight of himself now. The scars on the right side of his face were thick, wide, and deep. His sightless eye fixed and white. His ear half gone. His mouth ever so slightly drooping. A monster, he had thought bleakly the first time he had seen himself in the hospital. His sister's reaction to the sight of him had been the confirmation of all his worst fears.

"Wouldn't you?" he asked.

She looked at him fully then, her blue gaze drifting over his face, taking in each sign of disfigurement with an unflinching steadiness that left him feeling shaken and exposed. "Perhaps," she said. "But it is different for a woman."

"Ah."

"It is," she insisted. "A woman's value is almost always determined by her beauty. While a gentleman...A gentleman is valued for other things. His intelligence. His bravery. His skill at pistols or even at cards. I daresay that most who see your scars would recognize them as a badge of courage. It is how I view them. And I am generally thought to be a sensible person—despite recent evidence to the contrary."

A badge of courage. He would have scoffed at such drivel were it said by anyone else. But the words, when uttered by Sylvia Stafford, sent a startling frisson of warmth through him. He cleared his throat. "You refer, I take it, to your attempt to climb my bookshelves."

"Amongst other things."

He was in his shirtsleeves. She was in her dressing gown. It was scandalous for them to be conversing together this way. Alone. Both in a state of undress at past two in the morning. A gentleman would advise her to retire. He would inform her that their present interaction may well harm her reputation. Alas, he was not feeling very gentlemanly at the moment. "Very well, Miss Stafford," he said. "If you stay the remainder of the month, it shall be as you wish."

"You will accompany us out of doors?" she asked. "In the daylight?"

His heart pumped in a sudden rapid, panicked rhythm. What the devil was he promising? "Yes," he said. "In the daylight."

"And for dinner, too. Like a proper host."

"Dinner," he repeated flatly. *Bloody blasted hell.* He ran his hand over the side of his face again, cursing the necessity of having this conversation. "Have your meals been so bleak without me?"

"Not at all. I only—"

"Yes. Yes, I know. You think I should make an effort. And I will, but... Regrettably..." He struggled with the painful admission even as he uttered it. "I do not dine in company."

"That can't be true. You took tea with us on the day of my arrival."

"A foolish pantomime," he said dismissively. "I allowed my sister to pour out a cup for me, but I did not drink it."

Miss Stafford searched his face. "Why ever not?"

He might easily have made an excuse, indeed, he very much wanted to, but something about the lateness of the hour and the intimacy of their conversation compelled him to be honest. "This scar, here—" He drew his finger along the scar that ran from his eye down past the side of his mouth. "It has deadened the feeling on much of this half of my face. Not all of it, mind, but enough that eating and drinking in company is...unpleasant."

Her dark brows drew together. He saw understanding registering slowly in the depths of her blue eyes. "Oh, Sebastian."

It was the first time he had ever heard her use his given name. It was startlingly intimate. His chest tightened on a rush of pleasure that was almost pain.

Was she aware that she had done it? He did not think so. And he had no intention of drawing her attention to it. "You needn't pity me," he said.

"It is not pity." She brushed her hand against her cheek.

Only then did he realize that several tears had fallen from her eyes. He groaned. "Please don't."

"I cannot help it."

"You can," he assured her. At least, he hoped she could. Her silent, dignified tears had a far different effect on him than the emotional dramatics of his younger sister. If she did not compose herself soon, he very much feared he would do something fatally ridiculous. Something foolish and sentimental like taking her in his arms and pouring his heart out to her.

"I'm sorry," she said. "I am not a watering pot. It is all just so overwhelming." She dried the last of her tears on the sleeve of her dressing gown. "I suppose you do not think I have a right to cry over you."

"As opposed to who? Julia?"

"Is there no one else?"

At one time he might have laughed at such a ridiculous notion. Now, however, he found nothing particularly humorous about her false assumption. "A woman, do you mean?"

She gave him a short nod. The candlelight shimmered against her hair, turning the chestnut strands to red and gold.

"There is no woman in my life," he said. "I have been alone here the whole of this last year with only the servants for company. And Milsom, of course."

"He was your batman while you were in India, was he not?"

"He was."

"And—after you were injured—he was the one who cared for you?"

"If by cared for you mean badgered and bedeviled, then yes. He cared for me. He cared for me so much that, at times, I was hard pressed not to murder him."

She looked at him, smiling faintly for a moment before her expression once again grew serious. "May I touch your face?" she half-whispered.

Sebastian froze. Had he heard her correctly? Surely not! "I beg your pardon?"

"I would like to touch your face, if I may." She blushed. "If...If you do not mind it."

His heart was pounding. "I do not mind," he said quietly. "But why...?"

"Does it matter why?"

His chest rose and fell on an unsteady breath. "No," he said. And it was the truth. A part of him had been longing for her touch since the moment he saw her outside the doors of his apartments. Longing for it in the same way that he had longed to hear the velvet sound of her voice. "No, it does not matter."

She edged toward him, so close now that her legs brushed his, the voluminous folds of her dressing gown pooling over his booted feet. She raised one slender hand to his face only to stop a half second before touching him. "Will I hurt you?"

"No." His voice was a raspy whisper.

And then she set her fingertips very gently on the scar at the side of his right eye. Her touch was warm and soft and heartbreakingly tender. He tried to concentrate on his breathing. An impossible task as she began to trace the path of his scar down his cheek.

Her face was mere inches from his own, illuminated in the flickering light from the candles. He could see every subtle shift in her expression. The slight movement of her dark brows, the tremor in her parted lips, the rosy flush rising in her cheeks. She smelled of violets. She had *always* smelled of violets. It was subtle, clinging to her skin and her hair, mingling with her own unique scent to create a fragrance that was at once both sweet and disturbingly elemental. The scent tugged at something deep inside of his chest.

Was this how her letters had smelled?

He felt a stab of white-hot anger. Damn Roderick Stafford! Had he been the author of these last three years of misery? If so, Sebastian fervently hoped the blackguard was roasting in hell.

"Does this hurt?" she asked, her fingers hesitating near his ear.

"No."

"You were scowling."

"Was I? Forgive me." He made an effort not to sound as if her gentle ministrations were rattling him to his core. "You may proceed."

She leaned closer, trailing her fingers along the ridge of his ear. "It was more than one saber cut," she observed with a furrowed brow. "This one." She traced slowly from his ear to the edge of his jaw, her fingers stopping at his shirt collar to rest against his throat. "And then this one." She brought her hand back to his eye and followed the thick scar all the way down to the side of his mouth. "Which was first?"

"The one on my face. The one that took my ear and nearly cut my throat came afterward."

"Who did it? Was it the same soldier?"

"A renegade sepoy. Yes. I believe so. Mercifully, I was stunned after the first blow and scarcely felt the second."

"You were on your horse?"

No longer content to trace his scars with her fingertips, Miss Stafford brought her whole hand to lay alongside his cheek. It reminded him, rather painfully, of the way she had caressed his face that last night in the Mainwaring's garden. It was a memory he had lived on for three long years. A memory which paled in comparison to reality.

"I was."

"Where did it happen?

"At the Siege of Jhansi in '58."

She moved the pad of her thumb against the right corner of his mouth. "Can you feel this?" she asked softly.

He swallowed hard. "Yes."

She stroked her thumb over the edge of his top lip. "And this?"

"Sylvia..."

"How dear you were to me," she murmured.

A deep tremor went through Sebastian's body. He bowed his head, eyes closing as he drank in her words like a man too long deprived of water.

"I am going to kiss you now," she told him. There was a distinct quaver in her voice. "Just here." She leaned forward and pressed her lips to the scar on his cheekbone.

Sebastian exhaled a shuddering breath.

"And here," she whispered, kissing the corner of his blind eye. "And here, too, I think." Her lips brushed the ragged edge of his ear.

He had been as still as a statue while she touched him, but as she feathered kisses back down the scar on his cheek, guiding him closer with a gentle pressure of her hand, the last thread of Sebastian's control snapped. With a low groan, he brought his arm around her waist, sunk the fingers of his free hand into her hair, and turned his mouth to capture hers.

It was a fierce, demanding kiss, filled with three years of bitter longing. Sylvia's lips gave way to it, parting beneath his. And then she melted into him, one hand still pressed to his cheek, the other coming to rest on his bare neck, her fingers twining in the dark hair at his nape.

He kissed her and kissed her. Exploring the voluptuous curve of her lips and tasting the soft, inner recesses of her mouth. The scarred edge of his own mouth was not entirely cooperative. He knew she must feel the awkwardness of it as his lips moved over hers. But if she did, she gave no indication. Instead, she was open and warm and pliant, offering him all of her sweetness. And God help him, he took it. All of it. Kissing her until he could not think a single coherent thought. Until he could scarcely breathe for wanting her.

She made no attempts to discourage his ardor, but she soothed him with her touch, meeting the searching heat of his mouth with soft, caressing kisses of her own. Kisses that told him that there was no need to rush. That she was his. That she had always been his.

"Sylvia," he said hoarsely when they at last paused for breath. "Forgive me. I never intended..."

She smoothed her hand along the hard line of his jaw. "It's all right."

He turned his face into her touch. "My God, I fear I must be dreaming."

"Have you dreamed of me?" she wondered.

"More times than I can count," he said. "It was the only way I could have you."

"I was certain you'd forgotten me."

"Never."

"Nor I you," she whispered.

He felt her arms curve around his neck. Only then did he tighten his hold on her, hauling her up against the broad expanse of his chest. "How I've wanted you," he said huskily. And then he bent his head and took her mouth again.

He had clearly run mad, he thought vaguely. But if he had, then so had she. She was returning his embrace with a full measure of passion. It was nothing like the careful kisses they had shared in the Mainwaring's garden. No. These kisses were fevered and intimate. The sort of kisses a man might give his mistress as a prelude to a thorough bedding.

Sylvia pulled back, breathless. "Sebastian…"

He gave a low, frustrated growl of acknowledgment. "I know. Much more of this and we won't be able to stop."

She slid her hand from his neck to cradle his cheek in the soft, feminine curve of her palm. Sebastian's eyes closed briefly at the feel of her fingertips scratching through his late evening stubble. "You do care for me, don't you?"

He made a choked sound of acquiescence, half laugh and half groan. "My God, yes," he said. "So much."

She drew back just enough to look at him. Her blue eyes searched his face. "Do you mean it?"

A flicker of regret stung at Sebastian's conscience. He had treated her abominably since her arrival at Pershing. It was no wonder that she doubted him now. "I mean it." He caught her hand and pressed it against his lips. "I am going to take care of you," he vowed.

And he would, by God. He was going to make it his life's work to take care of Sylvia Stafford. She would never want for anything again for as long as she lived.

"Take care of me," she repeated.

"I am going to give you everything. Gowns. Jewels. A carriage and four. Whatever your heart desires."

She stared up at him, her brows drawn in confusion. "I don't understand," she said. "You must know I could never accept such things from you."

"You can," he assured her. "And much more besides. I intend to spoil you shamelessly."

She shook her head. "Sebastian…"

His gaze fell to her half-parted lips. She looked as if she were about to say something more. To give voice to another objection, no doubt. He captured her mouth before she could speak, kissing her deeply, almost savagely.

For one endless moment, she yielded herself to the tender onslaught. Her lips softened beneath his, welcoming and sweet. And then she turned her face away from him, her bosom heaving against the hard wall of his chest. "It was not like this before."

He pressed a kiss to the side of her mouth. "No" he said, nuzzling her. There was faint amusement in his voice. "Three years ago I would not have dared be so bold."

"Because I was a gently bred young lady."

His mouth stilled on her cheek.

"But now I am only a governess. A manner of superior servant, as you said."

Sebastian raised his head to look at her. Good God, could she really believe that? Could she really think, even for an instant, that he had kissed her so passionately merely because she was some sort of inferior person? "Sylvia…" He moved to reassure her.

She drew back from him, setting both of her hands on his chest to hold him at a distance. "You did not call me Sylvia then."

He had a sinking feeling that something had changed. A subtle shift between them that he could not quite identify. "Nor did you call me Sebastian," he pointed out.

"But I did," she said. "In all of my letters."

Devil take it! Those infernal letters again. With a muttered oath, he released her from his embrace. She immediately withdrew to the opposite end of the settee. Her dressing gown was rumpled and her hair spilled all about her in a glorious chestnut tangle. She looked thoroughly tumbled. "I've already told you that I did not receive any of your letters."

"It doesn't change the fact that I wrote them."

"Whether you wrote them or not—"

"You don't believe me?" She was aghast.

"Sylvia, listen to me—"

"Why on earth would I lie about something so mortifying?" Her blue eyes blazed with hurt that was—he realized to his chagrin—swiftly turning to anger.

He raked a hand through his hair in frustration. The conversation was rapidly getting away from him. "I don't know," he blurted out. "Because I am the earl now. Because I have inherited my father's fortune."

Her lips parted on a wordless exclamation. "Is *that* what you think?"

"No," he said at once. "I mean to say...It was what I thought when you first arrived here, but I—" He broke off with a curse. "Bloody hell, Sylvia. A man cannot think straight in these circumstances. If you will but give me five seconds to—"

"Miss Stafford, if you please."

"*What?*"

"I would prefer if you ceased calling me by my given name. I'd rather not be familiar with a man who thinks I'm a liar."

Sebastian scowled. "It's a little late to worry about overfamiliarity."

She looked away from him, her cheeks flooding with color.

"And I never said you were a liar."

She drew her dressing gown more firmly about her. "It's all right," she said. "I am glad, really. Indeed, it is somewhat of a relief to know what you really think of me. I only wish I had known before I left London."

He stared at her. "You make it sound as if you regret ever having come here."

"Of course I do," she said. "I should never have accepted your sister's invitation. One cannot revisit the past."

He felt the truth of her statement like a blow to the stomach. "And tonight? What happened between us just now?"

"Why should I regret that?"

"Forgive me," he said stiffly, "did you not just intimate that I was the sort of gentleman who debauches his servants?"

"Debauches? No. But you must admit there is a vast difference between the kisses we shared when I was Miss Stafford of Newell Park and the kisses we shared now I am a governess in Cheapside."

"Three years have passed. We are both older. And we are not in a garden during a crowded London ball. Naturally the intensity of our embrace—" He broke off with a grimace, embarrassed by the turn the conversation had taken. "It has nothing to do with your being a governess."

"Doesn't it?"

"No, damn it all!"

"You needn't lose your temper."

"I am not losing my temper. I am trying to tell you that I meant no disrespect to you. If you regret what has happened between us—"

"I do not regret it. *I* kissed *you*, if you will recall. I did not plan to, but now I think on it…It provides a certain symmetry to our acquaintance. A suitable ending, I feel."

A dash of ice water could not have been more effective. "An ending," he repeated. "After what we have just shared? I think not, Miss Stafford."

She fixed him with a level stare. "It is not up to you, is it, sir?"

"The hell it isn't," he growled. "If you think I am letting you go after this—"

Sylvia was on her feet in an instant. "It is my decision and mine alone," she shot back. "I am a woman of five and twenty now. An independent woman. I do exactly as I please."

He stood, looming over her. "Do you, by God? And I suppose it pleases you to kiss gentlemen who are not your husband? Who are not even your betrothed?"

A fiery blush stole into her face. "If it does, it is no concern of yours!"

Sebastian's expression was thunderous. Had there been others? How could there not have been? She had always had admirers. And he had been gone from her life for three long years. It would be foolish to assume that there had been no one else. "You have made it my concern by your actions this evening," he said coldly. "My honor as a gentleman—"

"What of *my* honor?"

His jaw hardened. He had no idea why he was losing his temper. Jealousy? Frustration? From the moment of Sylvia Stafford's arrival his mind had been in turmoil. Her presence alone was overwhelming, but touching her and kissing her had devastated his senses. Muddled his brain. Damn it all to hell! *Had* there been other men? He could not get the thought out of his head.

"But I suppose," she said, "you believe a governess has no need of honor or…or dignity…or to be treated with r-respect—" She broke off abruptly, turning away from him. When she spoke again, there were tears in her voice. "How *can* you think I would kiss just anyone? Simply because I kissed you that night in the garden? And again tonight? I suppose you believe me to be some sort of conscienceless flirt."

Sebastian muttered a low curse. In one stride, he was behind her. He closed his hand around her upper arm. "You begin to be as infuriating as my sister," he growled. His harsh tone was tempered by the gentle, reassuring squeeze of his fingers. "Of course I do not believe that. What do you take me for?"

She shook her head. "I don't know anymore. I cannot think."

"You're tired, that is all. We both are." He turned her to face him. The sight of her tear-filled eyes tore at his heart. He moved his hand up and down her arm, attempting to soothe her disordered nerves. "We needn't discuss anything more this evening," he said. "But in the morning, you and I are going to talk about a great many things. We are going to come to an arrangement."

She looked away from him. Her small, slender body was stiff and unyielding.

"For now, I recommend bed. And perhaps a glass of sherry, if you will take one."

She shot him a fleeting glance. "Why must you be so dreadfully reasonable? Your sister said you were a brute and bully. Pray bully me, my lord. Threaten me. Throw a porcelain vase at my head. Anything so that I might hate you."

"You would prefer to hate me?" He was incredulous.

"Yes. It would be easier. Less confusing than" — she made a vague gesture with her hand that seemed to encompass the whole of Pershing Hall— "this."

"You are talking nonsense." He squeezed her arm again. "Come. I shall light a fresh candle for you and then you may go back upstairs to your room. You will feel better in the morning."

She gave a small, reluctant nod. "Very well."

He dropped his hand from her arm and went to find a box of friction matches. The branch of candles he had brought in with him was still flickering valiantly, despite having guttered. It cast a dim glow around it, leaving the rest of the library sunk into darkness. Sylvia's own candle had long since gone out. He replaced it with a fresh one, lit the wick, and turned to give it to her.

"The servants should all be in bed," he said as she took it from his hand. "Even so, it would be better if we left separately."

"Yes."

"You go first. I will remain here awhile."

She inclined her head to him. "Goodnight, my lord."

My lord. So they were back to that, were they? He sighed. "Sleep well, Miss Stafford. I look forward to resuming this conversation at a more reasonable hour."

Chapter Ten

When Sebastian returned to his bedchamber, he found Milsom waiting up for him. During their years in India, the loyal batman had perfected the art of sleeping for short intervals, always managing to rouse himself at the slightest noise or sign of movement. He did so now, emerging from the dressing room with upraised eyebrows and a rather impertinent expression on his face.

Sebastian pulled his shirt off over his head, exposing a bare back and chest that were riddled with scars. He tossed the garment carelessly onto the end of his bed. "Well?"

Milsom picked up the discarded shirt. "My lord?"

"You look damnably smug, Milsom."

"Do I, sir?"

"If you have something to say, say it." He paused. "Unless it regards Miss Stafford and myself. In which case, I'll thank you to keep your mouth shut."

Milsom's eyes danced. "I'll not say a word about Miss Stafford, my lord."

"A wise decision." Sebastian sat down to remove his boots.

"Except to mention that I took the liberty of enquiring after those letters of hers earlier this evening."

"*What?*" Sebastian glanced up. "Enquired of whom?"

"Miss Craddock."

"My sister's maid? What the devil would she know about anything?"

"It is only a trifle, my lord. And no secret at all. Hardly worth the effort of discovering it."

"Go on."

Milsom bent to retrieve Sebastian boots. "According to Miss Craddock, Lady Harker learned Miss Stafford's whereabouts from a Miss Cavendish who, in turn, learned them from a Lady Ponsonby. Lady Ponsonby employs Miss Stafford's former lady's maid. A woman by the name of Harriet Button."

Sebastian was instantly alert.

"I understand," Milsom continued, "that Miss Button was employed by Miss Stafford for many years and was very much in her confidence. She was also highly esteemed by Sir Roderick Stafford."

"And how did Craddock come by this fascinating information?"

"It seems that Lady Harker requires Miss Craddock to read the post to her each morning whilst she is…" Milsom cleared his throat discreetly. "…in her bath."

Sebastian grimaced. It sounded like Julia. She had never been a great reader. And she delighted in being coddled by anyone willing to do it. "Am I to infer that Craddock read this letter from Miss Cavendish?"

"Yes, my lord."

Sebastian rose and began to work on the buttons of his trousers. "You're right, Milsom. A useless trifle."

"As I said, my lord."

"Nevertheless…" He stripped off his trousers. "I require you to catch the train into London first thing in the morning."

"To speak with Miss Button?"

"Precisely."

"I thought she might be of use, my lord."

"You thought right," Sebastian said. Clad only in his drawers, he went to the washstand in his dressing room. "It was Miss Button who was tasked with posting Miss Stafford's letters to me."

Milsom paused in the act of draping his master's trousers and shirt over his arm. "You believe that she meddled with them?"

"It would seem so." Sebastian poured a ewer of cold water into the washbasin. He plunged his head into it, holding it for a moment, before raising it again to find Milsom at his side, proffering a towel. He took it and proceeded to dry his face and his hair. "I suspect the letters were never sent. I would like to know why."

"The reason seems plain to me, sir."

"And to me," Sebastian said. "But Miss Stafford won't believe her father had a hand in all of this without proof. She is loyal—even to those who don't deserve it."

"You want me to find proof that Sir Roderick was to blame?"

"I want you to discover the truth if you can. Whatever it is."

"I shall do my best to find out, my lord."

"You may as well take a small purse," Sebastian said. "Any former servant of Sir Roderick Stafford will not be averse to taking a bribe. I daresay they might expect one. And Milsom?"

"Yes, sir?"

"I want to know everything, no matter the cost."

Approximately six hours later, Sylvia stood on the empty train platform in Apsley Heath, her carpetbag clutched tight in her gloved hands. She was wearing the same dark gown she had worn on the journey down from London, the same mantle buttoned at her neck, and the same silk bonnet on her head, its ribbons tied snug beneath her chin in a plain, uncompromising bow.

It had been surprisingly easy to find someone willing to bring her to the station. She had simply gone down to the kitchens at dawn and enquired of the cook. Mrs. Croft was a motherly woman. A kind woman. One look at Sylvia's swollen eyes and tearstained face and she had promptly summoned an old manservant from the stable yard.

"John," she had said. "Best hitch up the dog-cart. Young miss here must catch the next train down at Apsley Heath."

"Yes, ma'am," he had replied.

The next thing Sylvia knew, she was seated behind the old manservant in a rickety little one-horse carriage hurtling toward the neighboring market town. He had asked her no questions, thank goodness, only speaking to her once to bid her safe journey at the train station. And then, with a tip of his cap, he had gone.

She was alone again.

Alone and bitterly disappointed with herself.

Last night, she had come within a hair's breadth of falling into the same trap that countless women had fallen into before her. She had nearly allowed herself to be ruined. And not by some random rake or rogue preying on innocent governesses—though that would have been terrible enough—but by Sebastian Conrad. The very gentleman who had broken her heart three years before.

The worst part was, she could not even blame him for it. The whole encounter, from its very start, had been entirely her own fault.

What in the world had she thought would happen when she caressed his face and pressed kisses to his scars? She had practically thrown herself at him! Naturally he would react. She would wager that any woman—whether duchess or scullery maid—who had treated him thus would receive the same passionate response. Sebastian was merely a man, after all. And she had been a ready and willing woman. A woman in her nightgown! She could die of embarrassment.

She walked the length of the train platform and then back again, her fingers clenched so tightly on the handle of her carpetbag that her knuckles cramped beneath her gloves. The wind was high and chill gusts stirred the dirt and soot from the platform around the hem of her sensible skirts. But she hardly noticed the grime or the weather. Nor did she notice the smattering of people beginning to mill about—ticketholders, like herself, waiting to catch the early train to London. She was far too restless and overwrought.

"*In the morning you and I are going to talk about a great many things,*" Sebastian had said. "*We are going to come to an arrangement.*"

How confident he had been that she would become his mistress! As if she were so madly in love with him that she would be content to have him in any way she could get him. As if she would tolerate being exposed to scandal and degradation and all for…what? The dubious distinction of being the kept woman of an earl?

Come to an arrangement, indeed!

As it was, no one would ever know that she had been compromised during her ill-fated trip to Hertfordshire. But if she consented to an affair with Sebastian, she would risk not only her reputation, but her livelihood. The Dinwiddy's would never permit a ruined woman to teach their young daughters. They would cast her out without a reference.

And what if she should fall pregnant?

Sylvia's stomach roiled at the thought.

It would be shameful. She would be shunned by everyone she met. No decent person would have anything to do with her. Worst of all, she would be entirely dependent on Sebastian's good will. He could cast her off whenever he chose. And with his volatile temper, who knew when that would be?

Yes, she told herself, the consequences of such a liaison would be dire indeed. That much she understood. What she could not understand was why, despite knowing how much she stood to lose in the bargain, she felt such an ache for Sebastian, such a terrible temptation to return to Pershing Hall and live with him however he would have her for however long as he would have her.

You are as reckless as Papa, she thought with disgust. *To even consider throwing your life away for the sake of a few moments of excitement, a few moments of pleasure.*

It had taken years to mend her heart when Sebastian had broken it the first time. Years to build a new life for herself. She could not put herself through it again. She would not. Because if she did, it would be worse. So much worse. Three years ago he had only courted her and chastely kissed her lips. Last night, he had crushed her to his chest in a fiercely possessive embrace. He had ravished her mouth with his. He had told her that he *wanted* her.

Heat flooded her face at the memory of it. She bent her head, shielding her blushes from view behind the protective brim of her bonnet.

A moment later, she was jolted from her self-recriminations by the roar of the approaching locomotive. She watched it chug into the station, a sense of numb resignation settling into her heart. It came to a stop alongside the platform with a screech of grinding metal. A handful of passengers disembarked. Sylvia waited with the other ticketholders while the porters unloaded their luggage. It did not take long. Apsley Heath was not a popular destination, especially at this time of day.

"All aboard!" the conductor cried.

She tightened her hold on her carpetbag and began to make her way to the second-class railway carriage. There was nothing else to be done, she thought miserably. Any future with Sebastian was impossible. And the revelations about their long ago letters to each other had not changed a thing. They were two different people now. From two different worlds. It was best if she returned to hers and resumed her life as a governess. It was the right thing to do. The *safe* thing to do.

When it was her turn to board, a porter stepped forward to take her elbow. She thanked him for his assistance and then, after one last, anguished look at the Hertfordshire landscape, she stepped onto the train that would take her back to London and out of Sebastian's life forever.

As a result of staying up the better part of the night, Sebastian slept until midmorning. When he awoke, Milsom was already gone.

So was Sylvia Stafford.

"A maid went to her bedchamber at half past ten with a breakfast tray," said Julia, "but her room was empty and all of her things were gone. I sent Craddock to enquire if anyone had seen her and—can you believe it!—she discovered that one of the grooms drove Miss Stafford to the train station in a dog-cart. At dawn!"

Sebastian had been sitting in front of his mahogany dressing table, attempting to knot his cravat when his sister burst into his room. It now hung loose round his neck, forgotten, as he listened to her in stunned silence.

"She will be hours and hours away by now. And all I have in explanation is this note she left for me on her pillow, which says—" Julia let out a short yelp as Sebastian swept it from her hand.

He unfolded it, reading Sylvia's words with something akin to desperation.

My Dear Lady Harker,

I am returning to London. Forgive me for not taking proper leave of you and your brother. I realized last night that it was a mistake to have come and wished to depart at first light. My life is in London now. As a governess. Indeed, I am very happy there. One cannot revisit the past, no matter how much one might wish to do so. It can bring nothing but pain. I hope you will understand and accept my apologies for any inconvenience my departure may have caused you.

Yours Sincerely,
Sylvia Stafford

Sebastian read it again, deeply shaken. *One cannot revisit the past.* She had said that last night in the library. Had she known, even then, that she was going to leave him? Had she ever had the smallest intention of staying? Of discussing their future together? He had not formally proposed yet, it was true. She had been far too upset. But surely she must have known his intentions.

Was being a governess so much more desirable than being his countess? And was he such a monster that she must flee his home in secret at the first light of dawn?

Good God, he felt like a prize fool.

Julia fluttered around his dressing room wringing her hands. Her hair was still in its nighttime plait and she wore an elaborately printed dressing gown buttoned up to her throat. "If you will only finish dressing, you might ready a horse and go after her. You could still catch her if—"

"I am not going after her."

Julia watched, eyes widened in dismay, as he turned back to the mirror and yanked off his cravat. "What? I thought that you wished her to stay! And why aren't you getting dressed? Oh, where is Milsom? Milsom!"

"Milsom is away on an errand."

"Then I shall help you! Where is your coat? And a fresh cravat? You must hurry, Sebastian. I insist upon it."

"I am not going to London," he said roughly. "I have not left the estate since I returned from India. You, of all people, know why."

She reddened. "Yes, but surely you would be willing to go now. If it means you might win Miss Stafford."

Sebastian looked at his reflection in the central mirror of his dressing table. In the bright light of day, it was difficult to believe Sylvia had covered the heavily scarred face he saw with kisses. Indeed, the more he thought of it, last night seemed to him nothing but a wishful, desperate dream. "I am not going to London," he said again.

She spun toward the door of his dressing room. "Then I shall go—"

His hand shot out to catch her wrist. "You will do nothing of the sort," he said in a voice of dangerous calm.

Julia's eyes filled with frustrated tears. "Someone must fetch her back! I want you to marry her. And why can't you? Surely anything is preferable to being a governess in Cheapside!"

He visibly flinched.

"What did you say to her?" she demanded.

"Nothing." No, he thought bitterly, he had just kissed her. Held her in his arms. Told her that he cared for her so, so much. Bloody hell. He had panted and groaned over her like an uncivilized brute. How in blazes had he thought she would react? She had left the library in tears, for God's sake. He had probably repulsed her.

"You must have done else she would not have left! And I know that she was not frightened of your injuries. To be sure, she did seem a little sad, but she—" Julia's mouth fell open. "Oh no! Was it *my* fault? Was it something *I* said? But what *could* I have said?

"Aside from telling her that at any moment I might blow my brains out just as her father did?"

Julia jerked her hand away, making a dramatic show of rubbing her wrist. "Do you think it was because I said that I wished her to be my sister? To marry you and make you well?"

Sebastian groaned. "Good God."

"I admit, it did seem to alarm her. Though I told her right away that it was nothing but a foolish fancy." Julia's brow creased. "Do you suppose she has another sweetheart? She said that she was not married, but she never said anything about a beau. And she is ever so pretty, Sebastian. Which is even more reason you must go at once to Cheapside and fetch her. If she knew she might be a countess, I daresay she would throw over whoever it is that is courting her now."

He dropped his face into his hands. Again, the specter of those other men! Her suitors had cut her acquaintance after her father's suicide. He had been reminding himself of that fact ever since they parted last night in the library. But just because the gentlemen of polite society had shunned a connection with Sylvia Stafford did not mean that she had been sentenced to a life of lonely spinsterhood. She was a governess now, true. But a beautiful, well-bred governess. No doubt there was a line of suitors stretching from Cheapside to Mayfair. Solicitors. Doctors. Merchants. Gentlemen schoolmasters. Sebastian conjured them all in his mind, each one handsome and elegant, soft spoken and kind.

"Out," he said to his sister.

"But Miss Stafford—"

"*Out*!" he thundered. And as his sister scurried from the dressing room and out of his apartments, closing the door loudly behind her, he felt the mortifying sting of tears in his eyes. He swallowed raggedly against the bitter swell of three years of pent up grief and misery. The loss of Sylvia Stafford. The death of his father and brother. The loss of his friends and his comrades in India. The damage to his face. The physical pain and mental anguish.

He felt in his pocket for the lock of hair, closing his fingers tightly around it, as if it were a lifeline thrown to a drowning man. It had always had the power to bring him back from the abyss. But now, as he held it against his cheek, he felt nothing. Nothing at all.

It was merely a symbol, he realized. A lifeless, soulless apology for the real Sylvia Stafford.

And the real Sylvia Stafford was gone.

Chapter Eleven

Sebastian sat alone in his sitting room, sprawled in the upholstered mahogany armchair in front of the fireplace. A half-filled glass of brandy dangled perilously from his fingers as he stared into the grate. Somewhere amongst the black ashes were the remnants of the note Sylvia had left behind when she returned to London. He could no longer remember exactly what it had said. Since reading it, he had been somewhat the worse for drink.

And that was putting it mildly.

He had not left his apartments for three days. During that time, he had drunk more than he had in his entire career as a military officer. More even than in those first months after his face had been cut to ribbons and he had learned that his father and his brother were both dead. He had continued drinking until his head felt as if it had been cleaved in two with an axe handle. Until the painful memory of Sylvia Stafford had been numbed and the taste and smell of her obliterated by the fumes of strong spirits.

What his sister did during that time, he neither knew nor cared. She had been raised at Pershing and had friends in the area. Perhaps she was out making calls? Gossiping with their neighbors? Or perhaps she had gone off to find some other lady from his past to persuade back to Hertfordshire?

But there were no other ladies in his past.

He had lost his heart but once.

Not that he had spent the bulk of his two and thirty years living like a monk, though for the last years it certainly seemed so. He had never kept a mistress. He was a career cavalry officer, rarely in England and only then for brief periods of time. There had been the predictable dalliance with an opera dancer when he came of age. A buxom, red-haired tart who made it no secret that her favors were wholly contingent on the gifts that he gave her. After that, he had done what the other officers did. The occasional night with a willing widow. The occasional visit to a brothel—though he had disdained the rather shabby band of camp followers that serviced a great many of the enlisted men.

And then, three years ago, he had returned to England at the height of the London season. He had arrived in town in the company of another officer, the youngest son of the renowned society hostess, Marianne Fellowes, Countess of Denholm. An invitation was extended to him for the following night. A musical evening, Lady Denholm had said.

"*Nothing too formal, Colonel Conrad, but I do like to encourage the officers to come when they are in town.*"

Captain Fellowes had been sheepish, but encouraging, assuring his superior officer privately that the evening would not be a complete waste of time. "*My mother always manages to find one or two distinguished performers amongst all the young chits strumming at the harp and shrieking Italian love songs,*" he had said.

Sebastian had arrived midway through the evening in his dress uniform, aware that it made him appear that much bigger, that much more intimidating. He had not been in the mood to exchange polite civilities about India. His attendance was a courtesy to Captain Fellowes' mother, nothing more. He sat in the back, grim faced, as he listened to a small selection of singers and musicians, most of which were—as expected—young ladies anxious to exhibit their meager talents.

But when the final young lady had finished on the piano and made her curtsy to the small crowd, a gentleman up ahead had risen to his feet. "*I say, Lady*

Denholm," he had called out to the hostess. "*Why have you not compelled Miss Stafford to sing?*"

A short, laughing exchange had ensued between Lady Denholm and several of the gentlemen in the audience. Admirers of Miss Stafford, Sebastian had assumed.

He had not been wrong.

Only then had he seen her. She was seated in the far right front corner, hidden amongst the enormous, full-skirted evening dresses of the ladies that surrounded her. She had stood, clearly embarrassed by all the attention, but not at all missish or falsely modest. She had an abundance of chestnut hair, artfully arranged with jewel-encrusted pins, and the bluest eyes Sebastian had ever seen. She had turned and smiled at the crowd. A genuine smile, despite her blushes, and one that revealed the presence of two bewitching dimples.

And he had been bewitched. Not because she was the most beautiful woman he had ever seen, though she was quite lovely, but because she fairly sparkled with warmth and light. She had given her admirers a look of good-natured reproof and then, after a word with the hostess, she had approached the piano.

"*Who will accompany me?*" she had asked

Not bothering to wait for other volunteers, a girl with ebony hair had emerged from the crowd and glided to the seat at the piano. Penelope Mainwaring, he would learn later. A diamond of the first water and Sylvia's bosom friend. "*What will you have, Sylvia?*" she had asked in a voice fairly dripping with fashionable ennui. "*A ballad? A folk song? A sea shanty?*"

Everyone had laughed at that.

"*An Irish Air,*" Sylvia had replied. "*Believe Me, If All Those Endearing Young Charms. Because it is short and we are all longing for our supper.*"

The gentlemen had protested, the most vocal of them demanding a lengthy love song. It had been the Viscount Goddard. A slight, somewhat pale aristocrat whose elegant form made Sebastian look a veritable oversized brute by comparison.

But he had not been jealous then. He had not known her well enough to be jealous. He had been merely bewitched. Merely enchanted.

And then she had begun to sing:

Believe me, if all those endearing young charms,
Which I gaze on so fondly today,
Were to change by tomorrow and fleet in my arms,
Like fairy gifts fading away.

Thou wouldst still be adored as this moment thou art,
Let thy loveliness fade as it will,
And around the dear ruin each wish of my heart,
Would entwine itself verdantly still.

She had a low, velvety voice. As merry as it was seductive. It had set a hook deep in his chest and commenced a slow, inexorable tugging. He had leaned forward in his seat, his eyes fixed on her. Her own blue gaze had drifted round the room, focusing on no one, as she sang:

It is not while beauty and youth are thine own,
And thy cheeks unprofaned by a tear,
That the fervor and faith of a soul can be known,
To which time will but make thee more dear.

No, the heart that has truly loved never forgets,
But as truly loves on to the close,
As the sunflower turns on her god when he sets,
The same look which she turn'd when he rose.

At the close of the song, he had approached Lady Denholm and asked for an introduction. And then, for the next two months, he had contrived to be everywhere that Sylvia Stafford was. Balls and supper parties, Cremorne Gardens and the theatre, picnics in the park, and even the damned circulating library.

Not that it had taken two months for him to realize his own intentions.

He had known that he loved her within the first two weeks. The remainder of his time in London was spent trying, by various measures, to determine exactly how she felt about him.

It had only been that last night in the Mainwaring's garden that he had dared press her. First by asking for a lock of her hair. Then by kissing her. Afterward, she had brought her small hands up to frame his face, rendering him almost speechless when she kissed him in return.

"*How many young ladies have you kissed in moonlit gardens, I wonder?*" she had asked.

"*None but you, Miss Stafford,*" he had answered her truthfully. "*None but you.*"

He had reentered the ballroom with her shortly after in a state of euphoria only to be instantly overtaken by the Viscount Goddard with whom Sylvia had, apparently, promised to dance the next waltz. Sebastian had leaned against the wall in the corner of the ballroom and watched them, resisting an almost overpowering urge to grab Goddard by his scruff and shake him like the impudent puppy that he was.

The next morning, he had left England for Marseilles, embarking on the overland route that would take him to India.

Once there, his duties had kept him busy from dawn until dusk—and frequently beyond. Skirmishes, both major and minor, had left him fatigued and often injured. The horrors of the rebellion had depressed his spirits. But Sylvia Stafford was never far from his mind. Of an evening, when they were bivouacked outside of a town or cramped together in some vermin infested cantonment, he had written to her. At first respectfully. And then, with increasing desperation.

It had been Goddard who had won her—or so he had thought when her letters never arrived. Sebastian had tormented himself with images of the two of them together, reflecting on the times he had observed them dancing or driving in the park. Realizing that she had never had any interest in a hulking cavalry officer at all. That, very likely, he had forced his company on her and she had been too polite to give him his marching orders.

But that had not been the case.

She *had* been writing to him. She had even been checking the papers, worried that he had been hurt or killed. And all the while, she had believed that he had been the one who was faithless. That he had ignored her letters. Or worse, been so offended by them that he had turned away from her in disgust.

Though what she might have written to offend him, he had no idea. There was nothing she could have said or done to drive him away. He had been half-mad for her. Yet, when they spoke in the picture gallery, Sylvia had seemed to be convinced that their relationship had ended because of something she said in her first letter. What in blazes could it have been? And why in hell would she think it would have been enough to put him off? Unless…

Unless she had written of some indiscretion with another man.

A sickening jolt of unease shot through him. Good God. Is that what it had been? Some confession about Goddard or another admirer? Had one of them stolen a kiss? Or more?

The thought was devastating.

And yet it made a great deal of sense.

She had told him that she had been very green and very stupid. She had apologized for her over exuberance. And she had said that she was deathly ashamed even to think of what she had written to him then.

Sebastian clenched his fist until his hand ached. It did not make a difference now, he told himself. She did not want him. Not even if it meant she might become a countess. She would prefer to remain a servant rather than spend one more moment in his company.

It was because of his scars, he had no doubt. Because she could not get over the horror of what had happened to his face. Because she found him ugly. Repulsive.

"*How dear you were to me,*" she had whispered as she touched his cheek.

The single sentence had been playing over and over in his head for the past two days. He had been deeply affected when she murmured it to him in the library, spurred on to take her in his arms and passionately kiss her. It was only now, in the painful aftermath of her flight back to London, that he understood the true significance of her words.

"*How dear you were to me.*"

She had spoken in the past tense. A fact he would have registered instantly if he had not been so undone by the sweetness of her caresses and the heady perfume of her warm, violet scented skin.

The past tense, Sebastian thought bitterly, because her feelings for him were in the past.

Nevertheless, if Milsom found some sort of proof about Sir Roderick's role in subverting her letters, Sylvia would have to be informed. She needed to know the truth about what had happened every bit as much as Sebastian needed to know himself.

He would not see her again, of course. He would not force his attentions where they were not wanted. And a journey to London was out of the question. Just imagining the reaction those in society would have to the sight of his face was enough to sap his courage.

No. He would not go to London. When he learned what Milsom had discovered, he would relay it to Sylvia in a letter. One final letter explaining all he knew of what had happened three years ago.

It would be a suitable ending to this whole painful affair.

Sebastian woke in the morning to the sound of Milsom moving about the room. He was making an ungodly racket. Clanging the water can against the washbasin, clattering the shaving implements, and unnecessarily flapping Sebastian's shirts about.

"Quiet, damn you!" Sebastian growled at him. "And shut those blasted curtains! Are you trying to blind me in both eyes?"

Unperturbed, Milsom brought him a tray on which sat a single glass filled with a brownish liquid. Sebastian recognized it at once as one of his valet's noxious tonics, guaranteed to alleviate the aftereffects of a night of heavy drinking. With a scorching oath, he drank it down and thrust the empty glass back into Milsom's hand.

An hour later, Sebastian was up, washed, dressed, and for the first time in three days, clean-shaven. Milsom had accomplished the whole with an infuriatingly smug expression. "Out with it," Sebastian ordered as he knotted his cravat.

"My lord?"

"You've been three days in London, Milsom. Unless you've expended the whole of it jug bitten in a tavern or unconscious in a brothel, I expect you have spent your time attempting to question Harriet Button."

"Quite so, but I was not entirely sure you would wish to know, my lord. Lady Harker has informed me that Miss Stafford left three days ago. And that you have since been confined to your apartments" —he cleared his throat— "drinking the cellar dry, I believe my lady said."

"I intend to write Miss Stafford," Sebastian replied coldly. He met Milsom's eyes in the mirror of his dressing table. "And when I do, I should like to have the full story. If you know it, Milsom, pray spit it out before I must assist you in doing so."

Milsom was impervious to threats. "As you say, my lord." He busied himself clearing away the shaving implements. "I *did* speak with Miss Button. It was not an easy interview to arrange."

"Hence the three days."

"Precisely so, my lord. Miss Button is almost always in company with Lady Ponsonby. I observed them for the first two days, awaiting an opportunity to approach, but it was not until yesterday that Miss Button set out on her own. She went to a chemist in Bond Street. I ventured to speak to her—a course of action which was not, initially, well received."

"I trust that the purse I gave you was of some help."

"It was an immense help, my lord."

"Well?" Sebastian prompted. "What did the confounded woman say?"

"Miss Button told me that Miss Stafford did, indeed, write to you. Twice a week for over half a year, she said. Once a week to follow. There were, according to Miss Button, nearly one hundred letters in total."

Sebastian's hands stilled on his cravat. He inhaled deeply. "Go on."

"Miss Button was under strict instructions from Sir Roderick Stafford to burn any letters that Miss Stafford wrote to you."

Sebastian had expected something in that vein. The letters would have had to have been destroyed, either by the maid or by Sir Roderick himself. Even so, he was shaken by the enormity of the offense. All those precious letters. Perfumed. Sealed with a thousand kisses. Letters he had waited for so desperately. "And so she burned them," he said quietly. "Nearly one hundred bloody letters."

"Miss Button was very loyal to Sir Roderick," Milsom replied. "To a point."

Sebastian heard a glimmer of self-satisfaction in his former batman's voice. He looked up sharply, meeting Milsom's eyes again in the mirror. "What the devil is that supposed to mean?"

"Miss Button is getting on in years, my lord," Milsom said. "She is consumed with worries over her impending retirement. A lady's maid does not make enough to put by, you understand. Miss Button has often been forced to secure the funds for her retirement cottage in Hampshire through other methods."

"Other methods?"

"Blackmail, my lord. It seems that Miss Button has long been in the habit of collecting various love letters and other incriminating notes from her employers and putting them away until they might be of use to her."

Sebastian turned slowly in his seat to face his valet, an arrested expression in his dark eye. "She would not have kept Miss Stafford's letters," he said. "Sir Roderick is dead and Miss Stafford hasn't the means to silence a blackmailer. There was nothing to be gained. This Button creature would know that."

"Exactly so, my lord," Milsom agreed. "Which is why she was willing to give this to me for a mere fifty pounds." At that, he reached into the inner pocket of his coat and extracted a small, faded rectangle of paper.

Sebastian's mouth went dry. "Is that…?"

"This, my lord, is the only letter of Miss Stafford's that Miss Button had kept. It is, I understand, the first letter that Miss Stafford wrote to you and the one that Miss Button deemed the most valuable. That she had not destroyed it in the last two years is the merest chance."

"The first letter?" Sebastian asked hoarsely. He reached out and took it with a hand that was suddenly damnably unsteady.

"The first letter, my lord. According to Miss Button."

Sebastian stared down at the gently swirling script that made up the direction. Sylvia Stafford's handwriting. "Did you read it?"

"No, my lord."

Sebastian raised the letter to his nose and inhaled. He could smell it, very faintly. Violets. He tightened his fingers around it. "You have outdone yourself, Milsom."

"Thank you, sir. Will you be needing anything else this morning?"

"No. That will be all."

Still beaming at his triumph, Milsom bowed and swiftly left the room.

Sebastian looked at the letter for a long time, his heart pounding in his chest and his pulse racing. It had been closed with a blob of melted red sealing wax that had long since been broken—no doubt by the blackmail-minded lady's maid. He was almost afraid to open it, but he was no coward. And whatever Sylvia Stafford had written him three years ago could have no real effect on the present, could it? They were only words now. Harmless, meaningless words.

He unfolded the letter and began to read.

My Dearest Sebastian,

I hope this letter finds you safe and well and pray that the overland journey to India was not too difficult for you and your men. Did your new horse settle? Or has he proved as temperamental as you feared? Captain Fellowes told me the sad tale of how your last horse perished in battle. I was grieved to hear it and know you must have been doubly grieved to lose such a fine partner. I wish with all my heart that your new horse will be as valiant and steadfast as the last.

As you see, I have asked after you, even humbling myself before the captain, who I know thinks me no better than a silly chit who has lost her head over a dashing cavalry colonel. I have tried to remain mysterious, but it is becoming very difficult. Lord Goddard is pressing his suit and I wish I might tell him why I must reject him.

My darling, I have been thinking of you often since last we met. There is so much more I wish

I had told you that night in the garden. At the moment it seemed as if I had already said too much. You mustn't declare yourself! Penelope warned me. He will run far and fast to escape you! Foolishly, I listened to her. I believed that I did not dare tell you all that was in my heart. Now you are gone and despite all my prayers for your safety, I realize that there is every chance I may never see you again. What if something should happen to you without your ever knowing the full extent of my affections?

I love you. There, I have said it. I do not mind to be the first to do so. I love you. There is no one else in my heart. There has never been anyone else. And I hope when you return we might be married. It needn't take a week of your leave. We do not even have to call the banns. We can be married by special license and then I will return with you to India where I will happily follow the drum. I do not know why you did not ask me in the garden. I thought you would. Every moment I thought it and when you did not, I feared I had done something wrong. Was I shameless? Should I not have kissed you? You must write and tell me, Sebastian. I know you will say exactly the right thing to put my mind at ease.

I can think of nothing but seeing you again. What shall I do with myself now you are gone? There is no happiness to be had anywhere. How can I delight in wearing pretty gowns if you will not see them? How can I take pleasure in dancing when you are not my partner? What joy is there in singing when you are not there to listen?

My love, you must endeavor to stay out of danger. Do not attempt anything heroic. I would far rather you come home in one piece than earn some silly medal or promotion. Not that I would not be terribly proud of you on either account, but I cannot bear to contemplate losing you. I have come to think of you as the only solid, reliable thing in my world.

Papa says I must continue to attend the parties here in town and let the Viscount Goddard drive me in the park on occasion. He says I must, on no account, look as if I am pining. But I am pining, Sebastian. Desperately.

I close this letter with a thousand sweet kisses. When I write again, I shall send you one thousand more. I have an endless supply of them for you, my love. Pray keep safe and come back to me.

I remain your own,
Sylvia Stafford

Sebastian did not know how long he sat there, reading and re-reading Sylvia Stafford's letter. At some point, he must have retrieved her lock of hair from his pocket, for when he began to return to his senses, it was clutched in his hand, his thumb stroking it in the old, familiar way.

I love you, she had written. And *I hope when you return we might be married.*

This then was what she believed had driven him away. A letter wherein she had exposed the innermost secrets of her heart. A letter full of endearments and affection. *My love*, she had called him. And *my darling*. A letter sealed with a thousand sweet kisses only for him.

He had been a humorless, stern-faced cavalry officer. A second son of little fortune and even less finer feeling. Yet she had loved him. And she believed he had read this letter and been unmoved. No, not unmoved. Repelled! That cursed Penelope Mainwaring had warned her of the very thing. *You mustn't declare yourself! He will run far and fast to escape you!*

Sebastian swore low and foul. And then he summoned Milsom.

"Fetch my sister," he said brusquely. "And then you may start packing."

Milsom lifted his brows. "Will we be departing for London immediately, my lord?" he asked. "Or do you require additional time to write to Miss Stafford?"

Sebastian cast his valet an ominous glance. "You are impertinent, Milsom," he said as he carefully placed Sylvia's letter and lock of hair into his pocket. "But the answer is yes, damn you. We will leave for London as soon as Lady Harker can make herself ready. The time for letter writing is over."

Chapter Twelve

London, England
Spring, 1860

"And then what did you do, Miss Stafford?" Cora Dinwiddy asked in an awe-filled whisper.

Sylvia looked across the schoolroom at her two flaxen-haired charges. The girls had been relieved to have her back so soon. Their mother was a kind lady, but easily overwhelmed by the high spirits of her two exuberant offspring. By the end of the first day, she had retired to bed, leaving the girls in the care of the already harried housekeeper.

"*Not a moment too soon, Miss Stafford!*" Mrs. Poole had exclaimed upon Sylvia's arrival at the door three days earlier. "'*A month!' I says to the mistress. 'You let the governess go a month without a by your leave? And what's to become of the house while I'm chasing after those two little devils?' But you know the mistress. She spends a half hour trying to herd those children together for a bit of sewing and then off she goes to her rooms with a megrim! And who do you think is left to tend things? It's myself, isn't it. But they don't want sewing. Oh no. They must have stories. And I'm to read them just as Miss Stafford does. Have you ever heard of such a thing?"*

Sylvia had found the girls in the schoolroom playing with their dolls amidst a great deal of disorder. The old piano was open, the music books scattered about. Crumpled drawing paper littered the floor. And someone—Cora, she suspected—had spilled their watercolors on the threadbare Kidderminster carpet, leaving an immense, bright purple stain that would have put the latest in aniline dyes to shame.

After a few stern words about their reported behavior and a polite request that they tidy the schoolroom in preparation for their morning lessons, Sylvia had left them and gone upstairs to her own small room to wash and change her clothes.

Had the house not been in utter chaos, someone might have asked why she had returned to London so soon or why she had arrived at the door in a hired hansom cab of all things. But no one had broached the subject until later that week. And the questions, when they came, were not from Mrs. Dinwiddy—though she *had* expressed regret that Sylvia's short holiday had not been a success—but from Clara and Cora themselves.

"Yes, Miss Stafford," Clara encouraged. "What did you do then?"

Sylvia used a piece of chalk to write a single word on the slate she held in her lap.

Earl.

She lifted it up for their perusal. "What do you suppose I did?" she countered. "Clara? Cora? How does one greet a gentleman of this rank?"

Cora frowned, staring at the word in consternation.

Clara, the elder, immediately brightened. "You curtsied!"

Sylvia affected to give this some consideration. "I certainly may have done if we had been in a ballroom and were about to dance," she replied, "but we were in a parlor just like the one you have downstairs. Would you curtsy to an earl there, do you think?"

"I would shake his hand," Cora said boldly. "I would say, 'How do you do!'"

Sylvia smiled. "That would be quite acceptable, dear, if he were an acquaintance of equal or lesser rank. An earl, however, is a person of superior position. It is his privilege to extend his hand to us."

Clara made a face. "I do not want to shake his hand."

"Indeed," Sylvia said. "He is not likely to offer it. Instead, he will bow to you and in return, you may incline your head, thusly, in a polite bow of your own. This will suffice for any person of superior rank, unless," she added with a solemn tone, "you should one day meet the queen."

Clara and Cora immediately went into rhapsodies. Sylvia, as always, endeavored to channel their high spirits into practical education. She lay down her slate and rose from her chair.

"Up you come, girls," she said. "Show me your best curtsies. You will need them if ever you are presented to Her Majesty."

The girls obeyed and, after a short, but spirited dialogue on whose curtsy was prettier and whether or not one of them might indeed one day meet the queen, they resumed their seats. And their questions.

Thanks to the gossiping servants and the unguarded tongue of their mother, Clara and Cora had always been extraordinarily knowledgeable about Sylvia's former life as a 'fine lady.' This, however, had been the first occasion that the household had had indisputable proof that once upon a time their very own governess had rubbed shoulders with viscountesses and earls.

Sylvia did not know what else they had been told about her trip to Hertfordshire. It was no secret, certainly, but she would rather not have discussed it at all. She had left Pershing Hall in an emotional fog, panicked and confused by what she had shared with Sebastian. As far as she was concerned, the least said about the experience the better. In time, she hoped her heart would hurt a little less. Until then, she was determined to keep herself so busy that there would not be a single moment free in which to fall into a blue melancholy.

"No more questions, girls," she said briskly. "We have wasted quite enough of this morning on the nobility." She used a cloth to erase the word *Earl* from her slate. In its place, she wrote a series of numbers. "Take out your slates, if you please, and we will address ourselves to a much more interesting subject. Arithmetic."

It was less than thirty miles from Pershing Hall to the Earl of Radcliffe's town residence in Mayfair. Only half a day's journey with stops to change horses. Had they taken the train, they could have made the trip four times as quickly. However, Julia was adamant that she could not disobey her husband's wishes in respect to avoiding train travel. Sebastian was skeptical as always of Harker's notions about his wife's safety, but he did not argue with his sister. Instead, he used the extra time to his benefit, explaining to his over-excited sibling exactly what he would require of her once they arrived in London.

"Harker won't like it above half," Julia said as she wiggled her toes on the hot brick that Sebastian had procured for her at the last stop.

He had forced himself to get out while the horses were being changed. Forced himself to go into the taproom and order a tankard of ale. The innkeeper had stared at his face, his eyes riveted to the scars even as Sebastian spoke to him. It had been a sobering experience. And yet, at the same time, it had been a relief. The innkeeper had stared in horrified fascination, true, but he had not appeared afraid and he had certainly not succumbed to a fit of the vapors.

Not that that meant anything. A rough innkeeper on the road to London was no doubt accustomed to unpleasant sights. The real test would come when they arrived in town and Sebastian was forced to interact with his peers.

"He will expect me to come home," Julia said. "I shall explain to him, of course, and I daresay he will understand. But you know how Harker can be, Sebastian. He was already quite irritable that I should wish to come back to Pershing so soon. And now, to tell him that I must stay with you at your townhouse..." She grimaced. "He will read me a lecture, I am sure of it."

Sebastian was gazing numbly out the window of the carriage, but at this he turned his head to look at his little sister. For all her silliness, Julia had been more than happy to accompany him on his impulsive journey, immediately dashing off a note to Lord Harker informing him that he was not to come to Hertfordshire, but to remain in London and she would meet him there.

He had been used to thinking of her as a confounded little nuisance. He had already been at Eton when she was born. Then came university and the duties of his regiment. He was rarely home and, as a result, had never really got to know her. Nor had he particularly wanted to. The brief moments spent in her company during school holidays or while on leave had been unpleasant in the extreme, filled with high-pitched chatter and youthful nonsense. His father and elder brother had spoiled Julia—praising and petting her for the very qualities which Sebastian deemed the silliest.

It had not occurred to him until now how she must have felt to lose them both in one fell swoop. And then to have her only remaining sibling return from India damaged almost beyond recognition. Yet she had continued to visit him at Pershing, forcing her company on him despite his grumbled threats and the occasional book or trinket thrown in her general direction.

And now, in what was perhaps the most affecting display of sisterly regard he had yet been subjected to, she had found Sylvia Stafford for him and unwittingly revealed a three-year-old misunderstanding that could, quite literally, change the course of his whole life.

"I will speak to Harker," he told her.

Julia brightened. "Will you? I must say, I think that is wise. There are precious few members of the family left, you know. And we must draw them all into the cause."

Sebastian resumed staring out the window at the passing countryside. He would have far preferred to handle everything on his own. Whatever happened next was between Sylvia and himself. No one else need have anything to do with it.

But that was the crux of the matter. If what he had in mind was to work, he would need the support of his friends and family, both of which were going to be a bit thin on the ground at present.

"Aunt Araminta and Aunt Sophie will still be in town," Julia said as if reading his mind. "And Harker's elder sister, Maria. And Lord and Lady Wilding. I can think of ever so many more." She smoothed a carriage rug over her flounced skirts. "I shall make a list and then we may send our cards round. They will all wish to call upon you, Sebastian. You are Radcliffe now."

"So I am," he said.

They arrived in the early evening, greeted by a skeleton staff who did their best to hide their dismay at the unexpected appearance of the new Earl of Radcliffe. Sebastian had not been to London in three years. The last time he had visited the townhouse, his father had been earl and his brother had been the heir. He felt a twinge of grief to see it now in all its stately grandeur. But there was no time for melancholy. He removed himself to the earl's chamber to wash and change, leaving Julia to take up the mantle of mistress of the house.

Geoffrey Randall, Viscount Harker arrived two hours later to dine with his wife. Sebastian did not join them for dinner, but after they had finished their meal, he convened with Harker in the library over a glass of port.

He had not been privy to the marriage negotiations between his father and Lord Harker; however, he strongly suspected that the late earl had thought to wed his only daughter to a gentleman of a serious and sober nature, capable of exerting some measure of control over her high spirits. To the untrained eye, Harker would seem to fit the bill. He was in his middle thirties, fifteen years Julia's senior, and a highly respected

Member of Parliament. But Sebastian had been evaluating the character of men under his command for over a decade and, though he was not insensible to his brother-in-law's merits, he could see plainly that Harker was the last person on earth to exercise restraint over Julia.

He loved her, poor fool, and as a consequence, indulged her quite shamefully. It was no wonder she was free to roam about the town calling on governesses in Cheapside and making up stories about suicidal elder brothers.

Sebastian did not know if his sister returned her husband's feelings. As a girl, she had fancied the golden splendor of Thomas Rotherham. While Harker was a man of, at best, middling looks, with a perpetually sad, drooping expression that put one in mind of a rather mournful bloodhound.

"Suppose I'll have to stay here," he said, frowning into his glass of port. "If Julia won't come home…That is…Can't very well command her, can I?"

"I need her, Harker," Sebastian said. "Without her presence…"

"Quite right. Quite right. Perfectly understand." Harker raised his head. "But you're not to shout at her, Radcliffe."

Sebastian was familiar with this particular lecture. Harker had delivered it several times before. "I have a temper," he admitted. "It has become somewhat worse since I came back from India. But I would not hurt my sister or any woman."

This assurance seemed to satisfy Harker. "Best thing for it is to marry, Radcliffe. Settles the spirits. Home. Hearth. All that sort of thing. I'm pleased to hear—" He paused, frowning again. "But I won't be precipitate. The situation you propose is…difficult."

"I take it you remember the scandal."

"Naturally. It was a shameful state of affairs. Stafford was accused of all manner of things after the fact. Don't know much about his daughter personally, but can't say I'm surprised she was blackballed. People were angry at Stafford." Harker shrugged and took a swallow of port. "With him gone, his daughter made a convenient scapegoat."

Sebastian clenched and unclenched one hand, focusing his slowly building fury into the small, harmless action, when what he really felt like doing was putting his fist through the wood-paneled wall. She had been all alone. And if he had only known, he might have helped her. "She had friends," he said. "Good friends. Lord and Lady Mainwaring—"

"Mainwaring, did you say?" Harker looked up from his port. "Sir Roderick was in debt to Mainwaring to the tune of twenty thousand pounds. Some investment scheme, I believe. Don't know the particulars, but you may rest assured that Mainwaring wanted nothing more to do with the situation. Can't imagine him assisting Stafford's daughter."

Sebastian looked down at his clenched fist. He had never liked Mainwaring. He was a baron who put on the airs of a duke and conducted his business affairs like a merchant. And that daughter of his! Sebastian had never yet met a female with such an exalted opinion of herself.

"Besides that," Harker continued, "he had a daughter of his own to worry about at the time."

"That should not have mattered. Miss Stafford and Penelope Mainwaring were friends."

"Lady Goddard now."

"*What?*"

"Mainwaring's daughter, Penelope. She's Lady Goddard now. Married Viscount Goddard two years ago. Not too long after Stafford's suicide, if I recall."

"Did she, by God," Sebastian murmured. So that was it, was it? A word from Penelope Mainwaring might have kept Sylvia in London; allowed her to remain with Lord and Lady Mainwaring. But instead Miss Mainwaring had taken advantage of the opportunity to rid herself of a rival.

"What's that?" Harker asked.

"Three years ago, Goddard was devoted to Miss Stafford."

"Ah." Harker gave a knowing nod. "More to Miss Stafford's exile than the actions of her father, then. Jealousy, perhaps? You never can tell with the ladies. Vicious as vipers, some of them. Would as soon sink their teeth into a friend as a foe. And Lady Goddard is a particularly formidable female. Daresay she'll be part of the contingent that calls upon you tomorrow morning."

Sebastian had wondered why Lord Goddard had not come to Sylvia's aid. Was this the answer? Had Penelope Mainwaring been hissing poison into Goddard's ear? Convincing him to give up Sylvia and take her instead? They had been her *friends*. And now, here they were in town—a viscount and his particularly formidable lady—while Sylvia Stafford was working as a governess in Cheapside! For two pins, Sebastian would have happily throttled the pair of them.

"Lady Goddard may await my pleasure," he said coldly. "Tomorrow morning, my sister and I will be otherwise engaged."

At half past one the following day, Sebastian was sitting in the front parlor of a small, but respectable house in Cheapside. Julia sat beside him on the overstuffed sofa and, across from them both, fidgeting nervously in an armless, button-back chair, sat Mrs. Dinwiddy. She was a short, plump woman clad in a dark silk dress with skirts that nearly rivalled Julia's in size. Her eyes drifted repeatedly to the scarred side of Sebastian's face. He was tempted to turn his head at an angle so his injuries were not so visible, but pride prevented him from making even the smallest concession. Instead, he looked his hostess directly in the eye.

He had arrived with his sister ten minutes earlier in a carriage bearing the Radcliffe coat of arms. The front door had been opened by another portly woman—the housekeeper, he had assumed. She had stared at Sebastian's face, slack jawed, before nearly falling into a swoon after looking at his card. After a series of curtsies that were painful to behold, and a few babbled mutterings of "your grace," she had guided them into the parlor and summoned her mistress.

"I do not know what is keeping them," Mrs. Dinwiddy tittered for what must be the third time. "They were only walking to the park. Shall I—" Her eyes strayed again to Sebastian's scars. "Shall I send someone to fetch them back?"

"Do not distress yourself, ma'am," Julia said. "We are quite content to wait."

"As you wish, my lady." Mrs. Dinwiddy clasped her hands tightly in her lap. "Though I never would have imagined when we hired Miss Stafford—" She gave another nervous laugh. "To think that I should be receiving both a viscountess and an earl in my own parlor!" She gestured about her as if to indicate the inadequacy of the stuffed sofa and chairs, the needlepoint pillows, and the profusion of blue and white china. "I am all at sixes and sevens."

Sebastian had been called upon to talk with people of all classes while in the army. He had not been especially good at it. He was far too gruff. But this woman, as silly and gauche as she was, had been kind to Sylvia. She had taken her in and given her a position. What might have happened to her otherwise, he shuddered to think. "I beg your pardon, ma'am," he said, "did you not know that Miss Stafford is herself the daughter of a baronet?"

Mrs. Dinwiddy pursed her lips. "As to that, my lord...She did say when we hired her how she had once moved in society, but that her father had"—her voice dropped to a whisper— "taken his own life." She looked from Sebastian to Julia. "Such a shocking business. I did not like to press her for the details."

"Naturally not," said Julia.

"Even if I had done, Miss Stafford was in no state to answer questions about her people. If you had only heard her voice when she recited her qualifications. So small and soft! Telling me about her experience with globes and painting and how she could speak tolerable French. Poor dear. She fairly shook. It was grief, you must understand. And no chance to mourn! Not but that I didn't allow her to wear black the first year. Though Mr. Dinwiddy did not approve of it."

Julia leaned forward in her seat, giving the older woman a look of sympathy. "Was she very grieved, ma'am?"

"Oh my, yes. And so thin and pale! 'We must fatten her up,' I told cook." Mrs. Dinwiddy smiled fondly at the memory. "She is the dearest girl, my lady. And such a way with the children. I have often been sorry that she has no family to go to at Christmas and no one to call upon her here, but she assures me that she is content."

Sebastian listened to Mrs. Dinwiddy describing the state Sylvia was in when she had come to them and felt the same sense of helpless fury he had felt when Milsom told him that Miss Button had burned nearly one hundred letters. Sylvia had not told him everything, he realized. Nor why should she have? As far as she knew, he was an unreliable gentleman who had callously ignored her. Why would she burden him with the knowledge that she had been pale and thin and crippled with grief?

"She keeps very busy," Mrs. Dinwiddy went on. "Only yesterday, she attended to the marketing with

Millie, our housemaid. And the day before that, why you would not credit it, my lady, but she carried up the mending to her room and in the morning she had completed it all!"

Melancholy was no match for industry, she had told him. Is that what she did now? Kept herself busy at all hours as if she were a bloody maid of all work in order to shield herself from the misery of her reduced circumstances? The very idea made Sebastian want to howl with outrage.

"We must convince her to have a rest," Julia said firmly. "Beginning with a drive this afternoon. You must insist upon it, Mrs. Dinwiddy."

Mrs. Dinwiddy nodded obediently. "I will tell her, my lady. I did hope she would stay in the country with you a bit longer, though I cannot deny that her return home was a godsend. My megrims, you know. And Mrs. Poole is not as skillful with the girls. Why, I've often—" She broke off at the unmistakable sound of the front door opening. "Ah!" she exclaimed with relief. "That will be them at last."

Sebastian's pulse quickened. He stood from his chair, giving one uncharacteristically agitated tug to smooth his black waistcoat. He was not naturally a gentleman prone to unsteadiness of the nerves. Indeed, he had frequently been accused of having ice in his veins. But hearing Sylvia's voice echo out in the hall, knowing now what she had written to him in that letter, he felt more nervous that he had ever felt before in his entire life.

"Do you each have your leaf intact?" she was asking.

The high-pitched squeaks of two little girls answered, followed by what was, unmistakably, a childish sob of anguish.

"Oh, my dear," he heard Sylvia respond. "Don't fret. Give that to me. Now take this in its place. You see why I gathered two extra? We must always plan for these sorts of catastrophes."

Mrs. Dinwiddy rose from her chair and went to the door of the parlor. She cracked it open. "Mrs. Poole? Take Clara and Cora up to the schoolroom. Miss Stafford? Join us, if you please."

Sylvia entered a moment later looking flushed. Her thick hair was pinned up in an untidy braided coil, the hem of her modest gray gown a bit smudged with dirt. Her eyes flew straight to his. She stilled, color rising in her face. "Lord Radcliffe!"

Sebastian was frozen where he stood. "Miss Stafford," he said. It was all he could do to offer her a bow.

Thank goodness for Julia. Before the silence could become awkward, she was on her feet and rushing at Sylvia with outstretched hands.

"My dear Miss Stafford." She clasped her hands and pressed a kiss to her cheek. "Were those the two little girls that you teach? How very energetic they sounded! But whatever was the matter? I hope no one was hurt?"

Sylvia gave Julia a bewildered look. "Hurt? Oh no, Lady Harker. No indeed. We... We have been collecting leaves to trace for our art project this afternoon. Cora's crumbled in her hand. She was a bit distraught..." Her gaze flickered back to his, her blue eyes uncertain. "Forgive me, but I had not expected—"

"Lady Harker and Lord Radcliffe have come to call on you," Mrs. Dinwiddy interrupted with a brittle laugh, "and have been made to settle for my company this last quarter of an hour!"

"We are come to take you for a drive with us, Miss Stafford," Julia said. "Will you need to change your gown or repair your hair before we leave? Shall I come up with you to your room and help you?"

"A drive? With the two of you?" Sylvia asked weakly. She looked at him again, her blush deepening to scarlet, and in that brief moment Sebastian knew—he simply *knew*—that she was recollecting the passionate kisses they had shared in his library.

He held her gaze until she looked away.

"It is perfectly acceptable," Julia assured. "And Mrs. Dinwiddy has insisted that you come."

"That I do, Miss Stafford," agreed Mrs. Dinwiddy. "And you needn't fret over the children. Mrs. Poole shall manage them quite well while you are gone."

Sebastian watched Sylvia's face. He could see the battle she fought between a lifetime of good breeding and the instinct for self-preservation. When her expression composed itself into a mask of polite civility, he knew that good breeding had won out.

"Yes, of course," she said to Julia. "You are most kind. If you will but allow me a moment to change? I muddied my skirts during my walk with the children."

Julia cheerfully assured her that they had all the time in the world. A moment later she departed the room with Sylvia, chattering gaily the whole way.

Sebastian breathed a sigh of relief.

Chapter Thirteen

As if a drive in the park in a closed carriage were not peculiar enough, Sebastian and Lady Harker had arranged themselves on the seat across from her, one saying absolutely nothing and the other at great pains to fill the void of silence with an endless stream of trivial remarks.

Sylvia could not imagine why they had both come to London, let alone why they had both called upon her. Sebastian did not come to town anymore, did he? Indeed, to her knowledge he did not even leave Pershing Hall. And yet here he was. First in Cheapside and now in…

But she did not know where they were now. They had been driving for some time, navigating the city streets and, as far as she could tell from her brief glances out the carriage window, were nowhere near anything that resembled a park.

"I do not understand," she said when Lady Harker paused to draw breath. "What are you both *doing* here? Why have you come? I thought I explained..." She looked between them both helplessly. "Did you not find my note?"

"The one you left on your pillow when you disappeared without a word?" Sebastian asked.

It was the first thing that he had said to her since speaking her name in the Dinwiddy's parlor. Sylvia's heart thumped heavily in response to it. She had never thought she would see him again, nor ever again hear his voice.

"Yes," he said. "We did find it, Miss Stafford, and read your explanation for leaving us, too. Inadequate as it was."

Her lips parted. She would have liked to snap back at him, but found she could not. She had the sinking feeling that something was very wrong. That feeling was intensified when the carriage slowed to a halt. She peered out the window only to turn back to her two companions with an expression of mingled shock and outrage. "We are in Grosvenor Square!"

Lady Harker smiled brightly. "Yes, that's right. We are going to have tea in front of a nice warm fire. Does that not sound a treat?"

A footman opened the door of the carriage before Sylvia could reply. Sebastian exited without a word. He handed down his sister and then extended his large, gloved hand for her. The servants were all watching. She could not make a scene. Neither could she bear to see any of her former society acquaintance. "To whom does this house belong?" she asked under her breath.

Sebastian's face was rigid. "To the Earl of Radcliffe."

She drew back instinctively. "Oh, but you know I cannot—"

"The proprieties have all been observed, Miss Stafford. My sister is here, as you see. She is a highly respected married lady. You will be quite safe. Now, if you will allow me." Sebastian extended his hand again.

This time she took it, permitting him to assist her down from the carriage. Her heart was beating so rapidly she thought she might swoon. Tea? At Sebastian's own house? Surely this was not a good idea!

"The fire is blazing in the library," Lady Harker said as they proceeded into the marble entry hall. A sweeping staircase curved gracefully to the floors above and a magnificent gas chandelier hung from the center of the high ceiling. "It will be nice and warm." She divested herself of her bonnet and gloves and handed them off to a supercilious-looking butler.

Sylvia did the same, smoothing her frayed hair with an unsteady hand as she followed Lady Harker down the hall. Sebastian walked behind them at a distance. She did not even see him again until they entered the library.

It was indeed a warm room, the rich furnishings and dark paneled walls making it feel even more so. At Lady Harker's bidding, Sylvia seated herself on a sofa upholstered in striped silk damask. Lady Harker settled beside her. Sebastian sat down across from them in an oversized armchair, his large frame as taut as a coiled spring. She was not the only one who was nervous then, Sylvia thought. At least that was something.

"Oh dear!" Lady Harker leapt to her feet in a rustle of starched petticoats. "I have only just remembered about the preserves for our tea! I must have a word with cook. Pray excuse me a moment, Miss Stafford. I shall be back in an instant."

Sylvia watched in wide-eyed astonishment as Lady Harker darted out of the library. The heavy door closed behind her with a soft, but significant click. Sylvia stared at it for a moment, too stunned to speak. "She's not coming back, is she?"

"No," Sebastian acknowledged. "Not until I summon her."

Sylvia fixed him with an accusing glare. "And just what do you mean by this, my lord? You assured me that your sister would remain—"

"Never mind my sister," he said, his voice quiet but firm. "We need to talk."

"We might have done so in the carriage. Or in the Dinwiddy's front parlor. You needn't have brought me here—"

"We must speak alone. Without any chance of disturbance. It is the sole reason I have come to London."

Her hands were resting at her sides. At his words, her fingers tightened into the sofa cushion. "You came all the way to London to speak...with *me*?"

"You left me no choice, Miss Stafford. Had you remained at Pershing but a few hours longer we might have discussed this there. I confess I would have preferred it. I had not planned to ever set foot in London again. In truth, I had not intended to ever leave my estate. If you knew the pains I have gone through to see you again—"

"You should not have come," she said.

"Miss Stafford—"

"It is all too much for me, can't you see that? I am not part of your world anymore. To be here with you...in your own house and surrounded by all of these things. It makes me terribly unhappy. And I have worked so hard not to be unhappy. You cannot know—"

"I do not wish to make you unhappy."

"Then I beg you, please, summon your sister. Pray send for your carriage to take me back to Cheapside."

Sebastian's jaw hardened. "If that is what you wish, I will certainly do so," he said. "After you have listened to what I have to say."

She clasped her hands in her lap. "There is nothing you *could* say."

He looked at her a long time, his face grim. He was dressed just as he had been years ago whenever she saw him about town. Black, fine wool trousers and matching waistcoat, a crisp white linen shirt, and a fitted black frock coat that set off the magnificent breadth of his shoulders. Shoulders that were presently bunched with tension.

"I have discovered what happened to your letters, Miss Stafford," he said.

She stared at him, stunned. She had been expecting a proposition—a formal offer to become his mistress. Isn't that why he had come to London? "I beg your pardon?"

"You said that you had given them to your maid to post. Your maid who is now employed by Lady Ponsonby."

"Button," she said, hardly recognizing her own voice.

He nodded. "I sent Milsom to London to make enquiries. He returned yesterday after having talked to Miss Button. It seems that your father instructed your maid to burn all the letters that you wrote to me."

His words struck Sylvia like a physical blow. She pressed a hand to her abdomen, her breath catching in her throat. "She *burned* my letters?"

"All but one," Sebastian said, "which she kept back for future blackmail purposes, apparently. According to Milsom, your former maid is at great pains to secure a retirement cottage in Hampshire."

Sylvia swallowed. "Which letter?" she asked

Sebastian met her anxious gaze. "The first letter," he said.

She briefly closed her eyes as a fiery blush crept into her face. "The first letter," she repeated. "Of course it would be."

"Milsom bought it from her for fifty pounds. He brought it back to Pershing with him. I read it yesterday morning. And now I am here, Miss Stafford. I have come to tell you…that the overland journey was unremarkable. My new horse settled admirably, though I regret to say that I lost him at the siege of Jhansi. I love you. I have *always* loved you. And we may be married as soon as you please. I resigned my commission. You can no longer follow the drum, but I sincerely hope you will settle for being my countess. I did not propose to you that night in the garden because I was afraid of being rejected, damn me. You were not shameless and the kiss you gave me then sustained me through two years of hell." He paused, plainly shaken. "Forgive me, I did not stay safe. And I have come back to you three years too late and not in the best of looks, but I—"

Sylvia did not realize that she was crying until she heard Sebastian break off his speech with a muttered oath. In seconds, he was at her side on the sofa, gathering her up in his strong arms just as the first sob shook her frame. She turned her face into his shoulder and wept.

"Ah, my dear," he murmured.

The husky endearment caused her tears to fall that much more quickly. "H-how could he have done it?" she asked, choking back another sob. "All that t-time. When he knew that my heart was b-breaking."

Sebastian's large hand moved on her back. "Your father wanted better for you."

And for himself. The unspoken words hung in the air between them. Papa had told her she might marry whomever she wished, but it had all been lies. He had never intended for her to wed a soldier—not even a soldier who was the second son of an earl. No. He had wanted a son-in-law who was wealthy enough to pay his gaming debts.

"*He wagered everything in that last game,*" she had told Sebastian that afternoon in the window embrasure. "*I daresay he would have wagered me, too, if he had thought of it in time.*"

But he *had* thought of it. It was what he had been doing all along. Gambling with her life, with her very future, just as surely as he gambled over a hand of cards. All so she could have someone better. But not better for her. Better for *him*.

"There was no one better," she said through her tears. "There n-never has been."

Sebastian tightened his arms around her. She could feel the heavy thundering of his heart against her chest. He was soothing her, but he was far from calm himself. "You do me too much honor."

"It is the truth, merely. But Papa would not have seen it that way. If he was set on my marrying a fortune he would have been looking elsewhere. At Lord Goddard, I suppose."

"Very probably."

She pulled back from him with a sniffle, fumbling about her for a handkerchief. Before she could locate the one in her reticule, Sebastian pressed his own large handkerchief into her hand. She used it to dry her face and to blow her nose. It was all quite unromantic. "I have ruined your cravat," she said.

"To hell with my cravat," he replied.

Sylvia blinked up at him. How grave he appeared. As if he were waiting for something. "Lord Goddard proposed to me before Papa died," she confessed.

His expression betrayed a flicker of surprise. "Did he?"

"I told him that I could not marry him. That I loved someone else. '*Colonel Conrad, I gather,*' he said. And I said yes. That I was waiting for you to come home." She blotted the fresh tears that welled in her eyes. "If I had accepted him...If I had not been waiting for you...Perhaps Papa would not have been forced to such drastic measures. Lord Goddard could have paid off his debts. He may still be alive today if I had only—"

"I doubt it would have made a difference. And in the end...if you had accepted his offer...Would you have been happy as Lady Goddard, do you think?"

"I would have been miserable."

Sebastian reached out to smooth a stray lock of hair from her damp cheek. "And would you be happy as Lady Radcliffe?"

She exhaled a tremulous breath. "I am a governess now."

"Much that I care."

"You cared that night in the library."

"That you are a governess? My God, Sylvia...You can't still believe that what happened between us—"

"I didn't want to believe it, but...If you had thought me worthy of marriage you would have proposed that night. Instead, you spoke of...of making me your m-mistress."

Sebastian drew back, thunderstruck. "The hell I did!"

His reaction was so genuine that, for an instant, she felt a stirring of doubt. "But you did," she said. "You mentioned an arrangement and gifts and—"

A look of dawning realization stole over his face. "Is this why you left Hertfordshire?"

"Yes," she admitted. "I-I did not know what else to do."

"You might have come to me."

She shook her head. "I did not trust myself. Not after what happened between us."

His expression softened. He seemed to understand, to sympathize even. "You were overset," he said. "Which is precisely why I did not broach the subject of marriage that night." He brought his hand to her cheek. "Sylvia…I didn't want you as my mistress. I wanted you as my wife. I have always wanted you as my wife. Had you stayed until the morning, you would have known that."

She dropped her gaze from his, swallowing back another swell of tears. "You can't marry me. Not with my job at the Dinwiddy's and what happened to Papa. You are an earl now and I am—"

"You are the woman I love," he said gruffly.

"People will talk."

"Do you think I give a damn what anyone says? What anyone else thinks?"

"No, but—"

"Besides," he continued, "I have a plan."

Sylvia lifted her eyes back to his. "What sort of plan?"

"Sir Roderick may have been a complete rogue and his death may have been a scandal, but he was still a baronet and you are still his daughter." He dropped his hand from her face. His jaw hardened with resolve. "I mean to restore you to the society for which you were born and bred. Lord Harker and my sister will assist us, but there are others who will be just as willing. Julia suggests visits to the theatre and a few small society parties to begin with and then, at the height of the season, a ball. A betrothal ball, if…if you will have me."

"You would do all that for me?" she asked in an unsteady whisper.

"What? Go about in society do you mean?"

She nodded.

"If that is what it takes."

"Is it what *you* want?"

"Good God, no. I do not care what society thinks of your having worked as a governess these past two years. And I do not care what they say about your father. You need no redemption in my eyes. If it were up to me and no one else, I would marry you tomorrow morning and spirit you straight back to Pershing Hall."

Sylvia's heart beat a delirious rhythm in her chest. "Tomorrow morning? My goodness."

Sebastian looked at her intently. "Sylvia...." A faint flush crept up his neck, turning him red about the collar. He appeared suddenly, and quite remarkably, unsure of himself. "I know that I am not what I was—that the scars have made my face terrible to look upon—but you loved me once. You said that I was dear to you. If you will but give me a chance—if you will agree to be my wife—I promise to give you everything in the world you ever wanted. To do everything in my power to—"

She pressed her fingertips to his lips, silencing him. "You foolish man," she said. "How little you know me." Her hand slid up to cradle his cheek. "All I ever wanted in the whole world was you."

A spasm of emotion crossed over his face. "Is that what you still want?" he asked in a hoarse whisper.

For years, she had promised herself that if she was ever again in a situation like this, she would be restrained. Dignified. That she would never reveal her true feelings as she had in those letters. But as she leaned closer to Sebastian, breathing in the familiar scent of spiced bergamot and starched linen, such promises flew right out the window. Penelope Mainwaring had been wrong. Some gentlemen—even the strongest and the bravest—did require reassurance on occasion. She gave it now with all of her heart.

"Yes," she said. "My darling, yes. You are as dear to me now as you were then. Dearer still because of your scars. Because I know all that you have suffered to come back to me. But, much as I want you, tomorrow morning is impossible. Mrs. Dinwiddy will need at least a week to find a new governess."

Sebastian went still, his gaze sharpening. "What are you saying?"

"I am saying that yes…I will marry you. And I do love you, Sebastian. I have never stopped loving you, though I have tried very hard to do so. But if you truly love me…And if you truly do not mind—"

Her words were lost as he brought his mouth down on hers. She gave a muffled exclamation of surprise. And then she brought her arms to circle his neck and her lips softened under his. She knew she must look a fright, with eyes swollen and her face blotchy from crying. She knew she must taste of tears. But he did not seem to care. He kissed first her lips and then her cheek and then her temple, all the while holding her in an unyielding embrace.

A light tap sounded at the door.

Sebastian's lips stopped on Sylvia's cheek mid-kiss. "Julia," he muttered. "Confound her."

Sylvia drew back from him as she heard the sound of the doorknob turning. "I thought she would not come back until you summoned her?"

"That was the idea."

The door opened a crack and Lady Harker poked her head in. She was beaming. "I could not help overhearing!" She entered the library, shutting the door behind her. "Is it true, Miss Stafford? Are you really going to marry my brother? Oh, but you've been crying!" She hurried to Sylvia's side. "What have you done this time, Sebastian? Did I not tell you that you must be nice to her and say only sweet things?"

Sebastian looked as if he might throttle his sister at any moment. Sylvia impulsively caught his hand in hers. She felt his fingers close around her own. "If I have wept, it is because I am so happy," she said. "Your brother wrote to me from India, did he tell you?"

"He has said so, but he will not tell me what he wrote. And he says that you wrote to him as well, though he will not confide in me about the contents of those letters either. I do not know how I am expected to be a help when I have been kept so much in the dark!"

"You may be of help right now," Sebastian said. "Miss Stafford and I are going to marry a week from today. You may assist with making the arrangements."

"In a week!" Lady Harker clasped her hands to her bosom. "So soon? But then I must get started right away, for you shall have to have a wedding breakfast. And Harker will want to stand up with you, Sebastian. And I will stand up with you, Miss Stafford."

Sylvia smiled. "I would like that very much, Julia."

Lady Harker's face shone with pleasure. "How wonderfully it has all worked out!" she declared, moving briskly back to the door. "And to think if I had not come to London and found you, the two of you would have gone your whole lives without knowing about those silly letters! But that is of no account now, thank goodness." She let herself out, still chattering as the door shut behind her.

Sylvia looked at Sebastian, her lips quivering with laughter.

"My sister," Sebastian said disgustedly. And then he, too, began to smile.

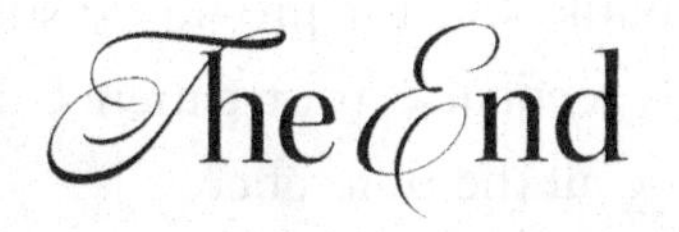

Acknowledgments

The bulk of novel writing is a solitary business; however, upon completion of *The Lost Letter,* there were many who helped to polish it into the story it is today. To them, I extend my heartfelt thanks.

To my literary agent, Nadeen Gayle, at Serendipity Literary Agency in New York, thank you for your unfailing support and positivity. Your faith in my writing means the world.

To my British and American beta readers, Sarah and Flora, thank you for providing such thorough and generous feedback. Your patience and attention to detail made all the difference.

To my friends, fans, and followers across social media and print, thank you for your readership. I love interacting with you all.

To my father, Eugene, who always supports me in everything I do. Thank you for all the encouragement and good advice.

And finally, to my mother, Vickie, who always reads my first drafts (and then submits to rigorous, deposition-style questioning), thank you for putting up with me. This story is for you, as promised.

About the Author

Mimi Matthews writes both historical non-fiction and traditional historical romances set in Victorian England. Her articles on nineteenth century social history have been published on various academic and history sites, including the Victorian Web and the Journal of Victorian Culture, and are also syndicated weekly at Bust Magazine, New York. In her other life, Mimi is an attorney with both a Juris Doctor and a Bachelor of Arts in English Literature. She resides in California with her family, which includes an Andalusian dressage horse, two Shelties, and two Siamese cats..

To learn more, please visit
www.MimiMatthews.com

Other Titles by Mimi Matthews

NON-FICTION

The Pug Who Bit Napoleon:
Animal Tales of the 18th and 19th Centuries

A Victorian Lady's Guide to Fashion and Beauty

FICTION

The Viscount and the Vicar's Daughter
A Victorian Romance

A Holiday by Gaslight
A Victorian Christmas Novella

The Matrimonial Advertisement
Parish Orphans of Devon, Book 1

A Modest Independence
Parish Orphans of Devon, Book 2